Stranger in Paradise

Stranger in Paradise

ROBERT B. PARKER

**Doubleday Large Print
Home Library Edition**

G. P. PUTNAM'S SONS
New York

This Large Print Edition, prepared especially for Doubleday Large Print Home Library, contains the complete, unabridged text of the original Publisher's Edition.

G. P. PUTNAM'S SONS
Publishers Since 1838
Published by the Penguin Group
Penguin Group (USA) Inc., 375 Hudson Street, New York, New York 10014, USA •
Penguin Group (Canada), 90 Eglinton Avenue East, Suite 700, Toronto, Ontario M4P 2Y3, Canada (a division of Pearson Penguin Canada Inc.) • Penguin Books Ltd, 80 Strand, London WC2R 0RL, England • Penguin Ireland, 25 St Stephen's Green, Dublin 2, Ireland (a division of Penguin Books Ltd) • Penguin Group (Australia), 250 Camberwell Road, Camberwell, Victoria 3124, Australia (a division of Pearson Australia Group Pty Ltd) • Penguin Books India Pvt Ltd, 11 Community Centre, Panchsheel Park, New Delhi–110 017, India • Penguin Group (NZ), 67 Apollo Drive, Rosedale, North Shore 0632, New Zealand (a division of Pearson New Zealand Ltd) • Penguin Books (South Africa) (Pty) Ltd, 24 Sturdee Avenue, Rosebank, Johannesburg 2196, South Africa

Penguin Books Ltd, Registered Offices: 80 Strand, London WC2R 0RL, England

**This Large Print Book carries the
Seal of Approval of N.A.V.H.**

For Joan: with whom I am no stranger

Stranger in Paradise

1.

Molly Crane stuck her head in the doorway to Jesse's office.

"Man here to see you," she said. "Says his name's Wilson Cromartie."

Jesse looked up. His eyes met Molly's. Neither of them said anything. Then Jesse stood. His gun was in its holster on the file cabinet behind him. He took the gun from the holster and sat back down and put the gun in the top right-hand drawer of his desk and left the drawer open.

"Show him in," Jesse said.

Molly went and in a moment returned with the man.

Jesse nodded his head.

"Crow," he said.

"Jesse Stone," Crow said.

Jesse pointed at a chair. Crow sat. He looked at the file cabinet.

"Empty holster," he said.

"Gun's in my desk drawer," Jesse said.

"And the drawer's open," Crow said.

"Uh-huh."

Crow smiled. He seemed entirely calm. But so much energy had been compressed into his physical self that he seemed ready to explode.

"No need," Crow said.

"Good to know," Jesse said.

"But you're not shutting the drawer," Crow said.

"No," Jesse said.

Crow smiled again. It was hard to say exactly what it was, Jesse thought, but there was a vague trace of American Indian in his features, and his speech. Maybe he really was Apache.

"Nothing wrong with cautious," Crow said.

"Last time I saw you was in a speedboat dashing off with a lot of money," Jesse said.

"Long time back," Crow said. "Longer than the statute of limitations."

"I'd have to check," Jesse said.

"I did," Crow said. "Ten years."

"Not for murder," Jesse said.

"You got no evidence I had anything to do with murder."

"Homicide during the commission of a felony," Jesse said.

"I doubt you could prove that," Crow said. "All you know is I was with some people, and then I drove away in a speedboat to escape a shoot-out."

"With a guy who turned up dead, in a boat that turned up empty."

"Can't tell you about that," Crow said. "I got off the boat five miles up the coast."

"So you didn't come here to turn yourself in," Jesse said.

"I got some business in Paradise," Crow said. "I come here to see that you and I wouldn't be scraping up against each other while I was here."

"Two of my cops died when the bridge to Stiles Island got blown," Jesse said. "Some people on the island."

"Yeah," Crow said. "Macklin was a bad guy."

"And you?" Jesse said.

"Pussycat," Crow said.

"You gonna be in town long?" Jesse said.

"Awhile," Crow said.

"Why?" Jesse said.

"I'm looking for someone," Crow said.

"Why?"

"Guy hired me," Crow said.

"Why you?"

"I'm good at stuff like that," Crow said. "The guy trusts me."

He grinned at Jesse.

"And," he said, "I know the territory."

"Me, too," Jesse said.

"I know," Crow said. "And if we can't co-exist it'll make my job a lot harder. That's why I stopped by."

"Who you looking for?" Jesse said.

"Don't have a name," Crow said.

"Ever seen him?"

Crow shook his head.

"Got a picture?"

"Not a good one," Crow said.

"Want to show it to me?" Jesse said.

"No."

"So how you going to find him?'

"I'll work something out," Crow said.

"What happens when you find him?"

"I report to my employer," Crow said.

Jesse nodded slowly. "As long as I have

you in town," he said, "I'm going to do everything I can to put together a case against you."

"I figured that," Crow said. "I say you won't be able to."

"Limitation is sort of complicated," Jesse said. "There was bank robbery involved, kidnapping, these fall under federal statutes. I'll talk to an ADA tomorrow, see what they can tell me."

"Ten years covers most things," Crow said.

"We're going to watch you all the time you're in town," Jesse said.

"But you're not going to harass me."

"If we can put a case together on you, we'll arrest you," Jesse said.

"Until then?" Crow said.

"We'll wait and watch," Jesse said.

Crow nodded. The two men sat silently until Crow spoke.

"You know about me," he said.

"I checked you out," Jesse said. "When you were here before."

"What they tell you," Crow said.

"Be very careful," Jesse said.

Crow smiled.

"Macklin was good," Crow said.

Jesse nodded.

"I wasn't sure anybody could take him," Crow said.

"Except you?" Jesse said.

"Except me."

"Now you know," Jesse said.

Crow nodded. They were quiet again. Both men motionless, looking at each other.

"You let the hostages go," Jesse said.

Crow nodded.

"They were all women," he said.

"Yes," Jesse said.

They looked at each other some more. The room felt charged, Jesse thought, as if a thunderstorm were near. Then Crow rose gracefully to his feet.

"I guess we know where we stand," Crow said.

"Stop by anytime," Jesse said.

Crow smiled and went out the door, past Suitcase Simpson, who was leaning on the wall just to the right of Jesse's door, and past Molly Crane, who was on the other side.

Crow nodded at them both.

"Officers," he said.

And went on out of the station.

2.

Molly and Suit came into the office.

"I remember him," Simpson said.

"I called Suit in from patrol," Molly said. "I thought extra backup would be good."

"What'd he want?" Suit said.

Jesse told them.

"Brazen bastard," Simpson said.

Molly and Jesse both looked at him.

"Brazen?" Molly said.

Suit grinned.

"I been taking some night courses," he said.

"You have no idea who he's looking for?" Molly said to Jesse.

Jesse shook his head. "I'm not sure Crow does, either," he said.

"He say what he'd do when he found him?" Molly said.

"Said he'd check with his employer."

"Guy like that looking for somebody," Simpson said, "not good for the somebody."

"No, it's not," Jesse said.

"Think he'll find him?" Molly said.

"Yes."

"Hard to make a ten-year-old case," Molly said.

Jesse nodded.

"Isn't he some kind of Indian?" Simpson said.

"Claims he's Apache," Jesse said.

"You believe him?"

"He's something," Jesse said.

"He's a hunk," Molly said.

"A hunk?" Simpson said.

"He's absolutely gorgeous," Molly said.

"Isn't he a contract killer, Jesse?" Simpson said.

"That's what they tell me," Jesse said. "Probably part of his charm."

"Probably is," Molly said. "It makes him sort of exciting."

"Not if the contract's on you," Jesse said.

"No, but there's something about how complete he is, how, what, interior, independent."

"Power," Jesse said.

"Yes," Molly said. "He reeks of power."

"I guess I better take more night courses," Simpson said. "I don't know what you people are talking about."

"He's a little like you, Jesse," Molly said.

"Except that I just reek."

"No. You have that same silent center. Nothing will make you turn aside. Nothing will make you back up. It's...what do the shrinks call it...?"

"Autonomy," Jesse said.

"Yes. Both of you are, like, autonomous," Molly said. "Except maybe you have scruples."

"Maybe he does, too," Jesse said.

"For fantasy purposes," Molly said, "I hope not."

"Fantasy?" Simpson said. "Molly, how long you been married?"

"Fifteen years."

"And you got how many kids?"

"Four."

"And you are going to have sex fantasies about some Apache hit man?"

Molly smiled at Simpson.

"You better believe it," Molly said.

3.

"I wish to have nothing to do with this," Mrs. Snowdon said when Molly showed her a picture of Crow.

"Have you ever seen him before?" Molly said.

"No."

They were in the vast Snowdon living room in the huge Snowdon house on Stiles Island. Mrs. Snowdon sat on her couch with her feet on the floor and her knees pressed together and her hands clasped tightly in her lap. Suit stood across the room by the French doors to the patio. Molly sat on a hassock across from Mrs. Snowdon.

She looks too small for the gun belt, Suit thought. *But she's not.*

"Was he here with other men when they looted the island," Molly said, "and locked you and your husband up in the lavatory?"

"Late husband," Mrs. Snowdon said.

Her blue steel hair was rigidly waved. She wore a black-and-red flowered dress and a red scarf, and a very large diamond-crusted wedding ring.

"Was this man in the picture one of the men?" Molly said.

"I don't wish to discuss it," Mrs. Snowdon said.

"Are you afraid?"

"My husband is deceased," Ms. Snowdon said. "I am a woman alone."

"The best way to ensure your safety is to give us reason to arrest him."

"I will not even consider it," Mrs. Snowdon said. "It was a moment in my life I decline to relive."

"Has he threatened you?"

"Threatened? He's here? In Paradise?"

"Yes."

"My God, why don't you arrest him?"

Standing by the door, Suitcase smiled without comment.

"If you'd help us," Molly said.

"I'm not a policeman," she said. "It's your job to arrest him."

"Yes, ma'am," Molly said. "But we're not allowed to arrest anybody we feel like. At the moment our only hope would be that he could be charged with participating in a capital crime. Otherwise the statute of limitations applies."

"He has to have killed someone?"

"Someone had to die in a criminal enterprise of which he was a member," Molly said.

"Oh, God," Mrs. Snowdon said. "Gobble-dygook. A number of people were killed, weren't they?"

"We have to be able to demonstrate this man's involvement," Molly said.

"Well, I'm not going to do your job for you," Mrs. Snowdon said. "What kind of job is this for a young woman? Why aren't you making a home for a husband and children?"

"I do that, too," Molly said.

She and Mrs. Snowdon stared at each other silently. Molly looked at Suit. Suit shrugged.

"I don't think you need to worry about him," Molly said. "He doesn't appear to have any interest in anyone from his last visit."

Mrs. Snowdon sat rigidly and said nothing. Molly let out some breath and stood.

"Thanks for your time," she said. "We can find our way out."

Mrs. Snowdon didn't speak, and they left her there, sitting in her iron silence.

4.

Jesse took Marcy Campbell to supper at the Gray Gull. It was June. They sat outside on the deck next to the harbor. It was still light and there was still activity in the harbor.

"Things not working well with your ex-wife?" Marcy said.

Marcy had platinum hair and wore skillful makeup. She was older than Jesse but still good-looking, and clearly sexual. Jesse knew that from experience. But he had also known it before he had the experience. Jesse always wondered how he could tell. He never did quite know, only that there were women who were insistently aware of their bodies, and of their sex. And somehow by posture or magic they communicated that awareness as insistently as they felt it. Marcy was the gold standard for such women.

"You think I only show up when there's a problem with Jenn?"

"Yes," Marcy said, and grinned at him. "Fortunately for me, it happens enough so that I see you a lot."

"Course of true love," Jesse said, "never did run smooth."

"You and me? Or you and Jenn?"

"True love? Both."

"Wouldn't it be pretty to think so?" Marcy said.

"I love you, Marce, you know that."

"Like a sister," Marcy said.

"Not quite like a sister," Jesse said.

"No," Marcy said, "you're right. Not like a sister."

The waitress brought Marcy some white wine and Jesse an iced tea. Marcy looked at the tea.

"Off the booze again?"

"Got no plan," Jesse said. "Tonight I thought iced tea would be nice."

"Got any other plans for the night?" Marcy said.

"Let's see what develops," Jesse said.

"Let's."

They read their menus, Marcy got a second wine, Jesse got a second iced tea. The waitress took their food order and headed for the kitchen. The shipyard next to the Gray Gull was silent now, and in the harbor the last of the evening boats were coming back through the gathering evening.

"Of course you remember the events on Stiles Island ten years ago," Jesse said.

Marcy seemed to immobilize for a moment like a freeze-frame in a movie.

Then she said, "When I was tied up and gagged and threatened with death by a bunch of cutthroats? Those events?"

"You do remember," Jesse said.

Marcy nodded.

"I wish I didn't," she said. "Forced to think about it, I also remember that you came and saved me."

Jesse nodded. The waitress returned with their salads. They didn't speak while she set them down and left.

"You remember one of them? An Indian? A man named Crow?" Jesse said.

Marcy again had a freeze-frame moment. It lasted longer than the first one had.

"My protector," she said.

"He's passed the statute of limitations," Jesse said. "But if I can get a witness or two to say he was involved in a felony that resulted in homicide, even if he didn't do the killing, I can get around the statute."

She shook her head.

"You won't be a witness?"

"No."

"Your protector?"

"Yes," Marcy said. "Stockholm syndrome, gratitude, call it what you will. I was lying on my back with my hands and feet tied and my mouth taped. There were five bad men in the room involved in a crime that would send them all to jail forever if they got caught."

Jesse nodded. "So they had nothing much to lose," he said.

"Nothing," Marcy said. "I was helpless, and they were free to do anything they wanted to with me. I couldn't resist. I couldn't even speak. About all I could do was wiggle. Can you even imagine what that is like?"

"No," Jesse said.

"That's right," Marcy said. "You can't. I wish I couldn't. I wish I could forget it."

"But they didn't touch you," Jesse said.

"No, because they knew that they'd have

to deal with Crow, and they were afraid of him. Even Harry Smith."

"Macklin," Jesse said.

"I know. He was Harry Smith to me."

"If he'd needed to," Jesse said, "Crow would have swatted you like a fly."

"No," Marcy said. "I can't bear to think about it if I don't think of him protecting me."

Jesse started to speak and stopped. He put his hand out and patted her hand.

"Okay," Jesse said. "You came out of it okay, and that was because of Crow."

"And you."

"Me later, maybe," Jesse said.

They ate their salads quietly. The waitress cleared their plates and brought the entrées. Marcy sat looking across the table at Jesse. She was tapping her fingertips together near her chin.

"He came to see me," Marcy said. "Two days ago."

Jesse nodded.

"He threaten you?"

"No," Marcy said. "He was pleasant. Asked if I was okay. Said he had some business in town, and thought he'd check on me."

"You believe that?"

"I believe what I need to believe," Marcy

said. "If I stop thinking of him the way I do, I can't stand to live with the memory. I can't be Marcy. Can you understand that?"

"Yes," Jesse said. "I can."

5.

Molly sat with Jesse in his office.

"Nobody on Stiles Island will say anything about Mr. Cromartie," she said.

"Neither will Marcy Campbell," Jesse said.

"Even though you questioned her all night?" Molly said.

Jesse raised his eyebrows at her.

"I'm a law officer," Molly said. "I have my sources."

Jesse nodded.

"She feels he saved her life," Jesse said.

"All the hostages do," Molly said.

"All women," Jesse said.

"I told you he's a hunk," Molly said.

"Maybe they're right," Jesse said.

"That he did save their lives?"

"Yeah."

"Maybe they are," Molly said. "Still, a lot of people got killed, including two of us."

"And the only thing I saw him do was rescue the women," Jesse said.

"The other people," Molly said, "people in the bank, homeowners, other business-people, they won't even say he was there. They're scared, afraid to re-involve with him."

"Don't blame them," Jesse said.

"So, we got no case."

"No," Jesse said. "I talked to Healy. No warrants out on him. I talked to my guy Travis, in Tucson. Nothing. Crow doesn't seem to have been detected in a criminal act since he left here."

"With enough money to retire," Molly said.

"So how come all of a sudden he's out of retirement?" Jesse said.

"Well, he isn't, actually," Molly said. "He hasn't done anything but come here and say hello."

"So far," Jesse said.

Suitcase Simpson knocked on the doorframe and came into the office carrying a large foam cup of coffee.

"How's the crime situation at Dunkin' Donuts?" Jesse said.

"Under continuous surveillance," Suit said. "I got a little news."

Jesse waited.

"Wilson Cromartie just rented a place on Strawberry Cove," he said. "You know who the broker was?"

"Marcy Campbell," Jesse said.

Suit looked disappointed.

"You knew that?" he said.

"No, but what other broker would he know in town?"

Molly smiled at Jesse.

"She mention that to you last night, Jesse?" she said.

"No."

"Odd," Molly said.

Jesse nodded.

"You saw Marcy last night?" Suit said.

"She won't testify against Crow," Jesse said.

"Despite intensive interrogation," Molly said.

"Intensive," Jesse said.

Suit looked at both of them and decided to let it be.

"So I figure he's planning on staying awhile."

"Give us more time to bust him," Jesse said.

"If we can," Molly said.

"Sooner or later," Jesse said.

6.

Jesse poured himself his first drink of the evening. The scotch whiskey looked silky as it slid over the ice. He added soda, waited for the bubbles to subside, then stirred the ice around with a fingertip. Jenn always used to say he should use a spoon, but he liked to stir it the way he did. He took a drink, felt it ease into him. He looked at his picture of Ozzie Smith on the wall over the bar. He wondered if Ozzie drank. Probably not, probably hard to do that backflip if you were a boozer. He raised his glass at the picture.

"I made the show, I'd be doing backflips, too," he said aloud.

His voice sounded odd, as it always did, in the empty room. If he hadn't hurt his shoulder he might have made the show. He sipped again. If he didn't drink he might be with Jenn. If Jenn didn't try to fuck her way to fulfillment. If he were smarter he'd have let Jenn go and taken up with Sunny Randall. If Sunny wasn't preoccupied with her ex-husband. If . . .

Jesse walked to the French doors that looked out over his little balcony to the harbor. He had no illusions about Crow. Whatever his reasons for letting the women go ten years ago, whatever his reasons for protecting Marcy, if he really had, Jesse knew that had he needed to, Crow would have killed them all.

Jesse's drink was gone. He walked back to the bar and filled his glass with ice. He poured the caramel-colored whiskey over the ice and added the soda. He stirred it, and walked back to the French doors.

But Molly was sort of right. Jesse didn't know if he and Crow were alike. But there was something about Crow that clicked in Jesse. Crow was so entirely Crow. He belonged so totally to who and what he was. Crow probably enjoyed a drink. Probably had no problem stopping after one or two. Probably didn't get mad. Probably didn't hate. Probably didn't fear. Jesse took another drink and stared at the darkening harbor. . . . Probably didn't love, either.

"He's not missing much," Jesse said to no one.

Even saying it, Jesse knew it wasn't quite true. If he didn't love Jenn, would he be happier? He wouldn't be as unhappy. But was that the same? What would replace the sense of momentous adventure that he felt when he thought of her, which was nearly always?

Jesse made another drink. The evening had settled and the harbor was dark. There was little to look at through the French doors. After he made his drink, Jesse stayed at the bar.

In a sense, loving Jenn wasn't even about Jenn. It was about who he was by being in love with her. So why not just let her do whatever she wanted to and love her anyway. What did he care how many men she banged? *Let her go about her business and I go about mine and what difference does it make?* He heard a low animal sound in the room. It was, he realized, him, and it had come without volition. He looked at his picture of Ozzie and shrugged. *Okay, so it makes a difference.*

Was it more about him than about her? Did he hang in there because he would miss the high drama? He knew he loved her. He knew she loved him. He knew they couldn't find a way to make it work.

"Yet," he said, and drank some more.

7.

Crow was at a corner table in Daisy's, having an egg-white omelet with some fruit salsa, when Jesse came in and sat down at the table with him.

"Care to join me?" Crow said.

"Thanks," Jesse said.

Daisy brought him coffee.

"You want some breakfast?" she said.

Jesse shook his head. Daisy left the pot and swaggered away. Crow watched her.

"Daisy Dyke," he said.

"That's what she calls herself," Jesse said.

"Wonder why?" Crow said.

Jesse smiled.

"She was going to call the restaurant Daisy Dyke's," Jesse said, "but the selectmen wouldn't let her."

"Nice she's out of the closet," Crow said.

Jesse nodded and drank some coffee.

"Can't seem to put together a case against you," Jesse said.

"Can't lick 'em, join 'em?" Crow said.

Jesse shrugged.

"Doesn't mean I won't put one together," Jesse said.

"You do," Crow said, "I'm sure you'll tell me."

"First step is to find out what you're doing here," Jesse said.

Crow nodded.

"Be how I'd go at it," Crow said.

"You could tell me," Jesse said. "Save us a lot of time."

Crow shook his head.

"We're going to stay on you," Jesse said.

"How many people you got?" Crow said.

"Twelve," Jesse said. "Plus Molly, who runs the desk, and me."

"Four to a shift," Crow said, and smiled.

"We can be annoying," Jesse said.

"I know that," Crow said. "You were last time I visited."

"You're staying awhile," Jesse said.

"Maybe."

Jesse poured himself more coffee. The two men looked at each other.

"You know," Crow said, "and I know, that you aren't going to scare me off."

Jesse nodded.

"I didn't figure I would," Jesse said. "But it was worth a try."

"I don't think that's why you came to see me," Crow said.

"Why did I?" Jesse said.

"You're just trying to get little sense of what I'm like."

"That why you came to see me, before?" Jesse said.

"Yeah."

Jesse drank some coffee. Crow finished his omelet and carefully wiped his mouth with his napkin.

"So?" Jesse said after a time.

"So you know I'm not going away," Crow said. "And I know you're not going away."

The tablecloth in front of Crow, Jesse noticed, was immaculate. No spills. No crumbs. It was as if no one had eaten there.

"Yeah," Jesse said. "That's about right."

8.

He was a smallish man with gray curly hair, pink skin, and a bow tie.

"My name is Walter Carr," he said. "I am a professor of urban studies at Taft University."

Jesse nodded.

"This is Miriam Fiedler," Carr said, "the executive director of the Westin Charitable Trust."

Jesse said, "How do you do."

Miriam Fiedler nodded. She was tall and lean and had horsey-looking teeth.

"And perhaps you know this gentleman," Carr said. "Austin Blake?"

"We've not met," Jesse said.

"I'm an attorney," Blake said. "I'm along as a sort of informal consultant."

"This is Molly Crane," Jesse said, nodding at Molly, who sat in a straight chair to the right of his desk. Molly had a notebook in her lap.

"We are here representing a group of neighbors," Carr said, "in order to call your attention to a problem."

Jesse nodded.

"You *are* interested, Mr. Stone," Miriam said, "I assume."

"Yes, ma'am."

"As you may know," Walter Carr said, "there is a plan being implemented to transform the former Crowne estate on Paradise Neck into an alternative school for disadvantaged students."

"Mostly Latino," Jesse said. "From Marshport."

"Paradise Neck is very elite. The streets are very narrow. The ocean impinges on either side."

Jesse nodded.

"There is no opportunity for expansion of the present roadways," Carr said.

"True," Jesse said.

Blake the lawyer had a deep tan and

snow-white hair worn longish and combed straight back. He was sitting quietly with his legs crossed, observing. It was an approach Jesse admired. Ms. Fiedler was impatient.

"For God's sake, Walter, the point is simple. The neighborhood cannot support busloads of unruly children coming and going in so narrow a compass."

"How about ruly children?" Jesse said.

Blake smiled faintly.

"Excuse me?" Ms. Fiedler said.

"Is it the number of buses?" Jesse said. "Or who's in them."

"Those buses will represent a huge traffic problem," Ms. Fiedler said.

She looked at Molly, who was writing in her notebook.

"What is she doing?" Ms. Fiedler said.

"Her name is Officer Crane," Jesse said.

"Whatever it is, what is she doing."

Jesse smiled.

"I don't know," Jesse said. "Molly, what are you doing?"

"I'm a female," she said. "I have a compulsion to sit near the boss and take notes."

"Notes?" Ms. Fiedler said. "This is an informal discussion. There's nothing here for the record."

"What record is that?" Jesse said.

"Don't be smart," she said. "I do not want any notes taken."

"Okay. But I'll probably forget a bunch of stuff," Jesse said, "without notes."

"I want to hear what she has written," Ms. Fiedler said.

"Miriam," Blake said softly.

"No, I insist," Ms. Fiedler said. "What have you written, young woman?"

Molly riffled back though the leaves of her steno pad for a moment, studied a page, and said, "No spicks on Paradise Neck."

Blake looked down. Jesse's face didn't change expression. Ms. Fiedler was horrified.

"How...my God in heaven...how dare you."

Walter Carr rose to his feet.

"We have said no such thing," he said.

His pinkish face had gotten much pinker. He looked at the lawyer.

"Is this actionable, Austin?"

Blake's face was serious, but Jesse could see the amusement in his eyes.

"Most things are actionable, Walter," he said. "This is not something in which I would expect the action to go your way."

"She has insulted us," Ms. Fiedler said.

"I think she's just kidding you a little, Miriam," Blake said.

"Well, I think she's insulting," Ms. Fiedler said.

She turned on Jesse.

"I want her reprimanded," she said.

"You bet," Jesse said. "How many kids are going to attend this school?"

"Twelve," Carr said.

"So," Jesse said. "A bus will deliver them in the morning and pick them up in the afternoon."

No one answered.

"Twelve of them," Jesse said. "Age?"

"Preschool," Carr said.

Jesse nodded.

"The worst kind," he said.

Carr didn't say anything.

"It is," Ms. Fielder said, "the tip of the camel's nose. It needs to be stopped at the beginning before the value of the Neck simply vanishes."

"Real-estate value?" Jesse said.

"All value," Ms. Fiedler said.

Jesse didn't say anything. The room was silent.

Finally Ms. Fiedler said, "Well?"

"Twelve preschoolers and one bus do not seem to me a public safety issue," Jesse said.

"That's not your decision," Ms. Fiedler said.

"Actually, it is," Jesse said.

"In a democracy," Ms. Fiedler said, "the people rule. You work for us."

"What a terrible thought," Jesse said.

"So you are not going to act?"

"Not at the moment," Jesse said.

Ms. Fiedler stood.

"You have not heard the last of this," she said.

"I was guessing that," Jesse said.

Ms. Fiedler stalked out without speaking again. The men followed her. Carr stared straight ahead. Blake winked at Molly on the way out.

Jesse and Molly sat silently for a time. Then Jesse said, "'No spicks on Paradise Neck'?"

"She was driving me crazy," Molly said.

"I sort of guessed that, too," Jesse said.

"Are you going to reprimand me?" Molly said.

"Worse, I'm going to punish you."

"You are?"

"Yes," Jesse said. "You may not talk dirty to me for the rest of the day."

"Oh, God," Molly said, "not that."

9.

Jesse sat with Suitcase Simpson in the front seat of Simpson's cruiser parked at Paradise Beach. Simpson was eating a submarine sandwich for lunch, taking pains not to dribble on his uniform shirt. Jesse was drinking coffee.

"Funny," Simpson said. "Whenever you're near the ocean, you have to look at it."

Jesse nodded.

"Always makes me feel religious," Simpson said.

Jesse nodded.

"I wonder why that is?" Simpson said.

"Got me," Jesse said.

"Make you feel religious?" Simpson said.

"Yes."

They looked at the ocean for a time. It was high tide and the water covered most of the beach. A few people in bathing suits occupied the narrow strip of sand above high water.

"Crow knows we're watching him," Simpson said.

"No reason he shouldn't," Jesse said. "Who's with him now."

"Eddie."

"Crow doing anything interesting?" Jesse said.

"Nope."

Simpson finished his sandwich and wiped his mouth with a paper napkin. He put the napkin and the sandwich wrappings back in the paper bag that the sandwich had come in.

"Mostly," Simpson said, "he hangs around. He has lunch at Daisy Dyke's a lot. He has a drink at the Gray Gull in the evening. Goes to Paradise Health & Fitness every day in the morning. Rest of the time he cruises around town."

"Walking or driving?" Jesse said.

"Both. Drives all over town. Parks sometimes and walks around. Why?"

"Might help us figure out who or what he's looking for," Jesse said. "Where's he walk around?"

"Shopping center, goes in the stores. Comes to the beach sometimes. Browses all the shops on Paradise Row sometimes. Watches tennis down by the high school."

"He check out the commuter trains?" Jesse said.

Simpson shrugged. He took a small notebook from his shirt pocket and read through it.

"Nope," Simpson said. "Haven't seen him do that. I check with the other guys, too, and try to incorporate their notes in mine."

Jesse smiled.

"Lead investigator," he said.

"Might as well keep things together," Simpson said. "Do it right, you know?"

"Suit," Jesse said. "If it were in the budget, I'd give you a raise."

"But it's not," Simpson said.

"No. He ever go down to the wharf?" Jesse said.

"Nope."

"Softball?"

"Nope."

"Maybe he's looking for a woman," Jesse said.

"Because of where he looks?"

"Yeah. I know it's a big generalization, but he seems more interested in places where you'd find women."

"I don't think you're allowed to think things like that in Paradise," Simpson said.

"Incorrect?" Jesse said.

"This place is officially liberal," Simpson said.

"Long as they keep the cha-chas out," Jesse said.

Simpson smiled.

"Yeah. Molly told me about that."

"Ms. Fiedler was down at the causeway the other day," Jesse said. "With a clicker, counting the number of cars."

"How many kids you say there were?" Simpson said.

"Twelve," Jesse said. "Preschoolers."

"Means a minibus probably," Simpson said. "Once in the morning, and once in the afternoon."

Jesse nodded. They both looked at the blue ocean for a while. Then Simpson grinned.

"They gotta be stopped," Simpson said.

10.

Jesse's ex-wife stuck her head into his office and said, "Hi, Toots, got a minute?"

Jesse felt the small trill of excitement in his belly that he always felt when he saw her.

"I got a minute," he said.

Jenn came in, dressed to the nines, and gave Jesse a pleasant but passing kiss on the mouth. The trill of excitement tightened into a knot of desire and sadness. The kiss was passionless.

"I am on an investigative assignment," Jenn said.

"What's Channel Three investigating this

time," Jesse said. "The resurgence of plat-form soles?"

Jenn smiled.

"Are you saying that Newsbeat Three is not noted for high seriousness?"

"Yes," Jesse said.

"This is a good one for me," Jenn said. "It's like hard news investigation."

Jesse nodded. The knot in his stomach held tight. He knew it would be there until well after she left.

"Our sources tell us that Latino gangs are infiltrating Paradise," Jenn said.

Jesse stared at her.

"Latino gangs," he said.

"There is gang graffiti on several buildings in Paradise," Jenn said.

She took some snapshots out of her purse and put them on Jesse's desk so he could see them.

"Our sources sent us these pictures," Jenn said.

Jesse recognized a couple. One had been on the side of the commuter rail station for more than a year. One had appeared on the back wall of the food market at the mall. There were two more he hadn't seen.

"Can you name your sources?"

Jenn shook her head.

"Does the name Miriam Fiedler mean anything to you?"

She smiled.

"Walter Carr?"

Jenn smiled again but she didn't say anything.

"Jenn," Jesse said. "There has not been a gang-related crime in this town since I've been here."

"Isn't that odd?" Jenn said. "I mean, Marshport is right next door. There are gangs there."

"Several," Jesse said.

"You don't think they might want to slip in here, sometimes, where the streets are paved in gold?"

Jesse leaned back a little in his chair. Jenn had her legs crossed. Her pants were tight. He could see the smooth line of her thigh.

"I never lived in a slum, exactly. But I worked in a lot of them in L.A. People who live in suburbia think every slum dweller yearns to live there, too," Jesse said. "But many people I knew liked the 'hood. Wouldn't want to leave it. Would die of boredom and conformity if they lived elsewhere."

"To me," Jenn said, "that sounds like an excuse to do nothing about slums."

"That's probably it," Jesse said.

"No," Jenn said. "I didn't mean that you were like that. But are you saying none of the gang-bangers ever cross the line into Paradise?"

"Oh, they come over sometimes. Mostly, I think, to sell dope to high-school kids."

"Can't you stop them?"

"Can I stop kids from buying dope?" Jesse said.

Jenn nodded.

"Or selling it?" Jesse said.

Jenn nodded again.

"No," Jesse said.

"You can't?"

"No," Jesse said. "But I don't feel too bad about that. Nobody else can, either. Anywhere."

"Are you suggesting we just ignore it?"

Jesse was silent for a moment, looking at her.

Then he said, "Are we on camera?"

"Oh, God, Jesse, I'm sorry. I don't mean to be inquisitorial. I just get so caught up in being Ms. Journalist, you know? Always ask the follow-up question."

Jesse nodded.

"I would like to investigate the gang thing, though," Jenn said.

She smiled. The force of her smile was nearly physical. Jesse always felt as if he should grunt from impact.

"Not a good career move," she said, "to go back and tell the news director that my ex says there's no story."

"No," Jesse said.

"Are you mad 'cause I was, like, cross-examining you?"

"No."

"I care about my job, you know."

"I know."

"It matters to me, just like yours matters to you."

"I know."

"I guess it makes me sort of a pill some-times," Jenn said.

"Everyone's job corrupts them a little, I imagine," Jesse said. "And you could never be a pill."

Jen smiled at him.

"Even your job?" she said.

Jesse nodded.

"What has your job done to you?" Jenn said.

Jesse was silent for a time.

"I guess," he said finally, "you could say it has narrowed the circle of my expectations."

Jenn stared at him and widened her eyes.

"You want to talk about that?" she said.

"Not much," Jesse said.

"Please," Jenn said. "I'm not being girl reporter now. I'm being ex-wife who still loves you."

Jesse felt the tension he always felt with Jenn: trying to control himself, trying to keep what he felt stored carefully away so it wouldn't spill out all over the place. He flexed his shoulders a little.

"It's pretty hard," Jesse said, "to believe in much. You can't prevent crime. You couldn't even solve most crimes if the bad guys would simply keep their mouths shut. About all you can aim at is to make your corner peaceful."

"But you keep at it," Jenn said.

"Gotta keep at something," Jesse said.

"You see too much of human emotion, up too close," Jenn said. "Don't you? People lie—to you, to themselves. Few people can be counted on. Most people do what they need to do, not what they ought."

"You know that, too," Jesse said.

"I work in television, Jesse."

"Oh," Jesse said. "Yeah."

They were quiet.

Outside Jesse's window a couple of firemen were washing their cars in the broad driveway of the fire station. Jesse could hear the phone ring dimly at the front desk, and Molly's voice.

"So what do we hang on to?' Jenn said.

"Each other?" Jesse said.

"I guess," Jenn said.

"And we're having a hell of a time doing that," Jesse said.

11.

The east side of Marshport butted up against the west side of Paradise. Marshport was an elderly mill town with no mills. There was an enclave of Ukrainians in the southwest end of town. The rest of the city was mostly Hispanic. There had been a couple of feeble efforts to reinvigorate parts of the city, but the efforts had simply replaced the old slums with newer ones.

Jesse parked in front of a building that used to house a grammar school and now served as office space for the few enterprises in Marshport that needed offices. He had driven his own car. He was not in uniform. He was wearing jeans and a white shirt, with a blue blazer over his gun.

The door to Nina Pinero's office had OUT-REACH stenciled on it in black. Jesse went in. The office was a former classroom, on the second floor, in back, with a view of a play-ground where a couple of kids shot desultory baskets on a blacktop court at a hoop with a chain net. The playground was littered with bottles and newspapers and fast-food wrap-pers and scraps of indeterminate stuff.

The blackboard was still there, and the bul-letin board, which was covered with memos tacked up with colored map pins. There were a couple of file cabinets against the near wall, and Nina Pinero's desk looked like a holdover from the classroom days. There were three telephones on it.

"Nina Pinero?" Jesse said.

"I'm Nina," she said.

There was no one else in the room.

"I'm Jesse Stone," Jesse said. "I called earlier."

"Mr. Stone," Nina said. She nodded at a straight chair next to the desk. "Have a seat."

Jesse sat.

"Tell me about your plans for the Crowne estate in Paradise," Jesse said, "if you would."

"So you can figure out how to prevent us?" Nina Pinero said.

"So we can avoid any incivility," Jesse said.

"Latinos are uncivilized?" Nina Pinero said.

"I was thinking more about the folks in Paradise," Jesse said.

She was slim and strong-looking, as if she worked out. Her hair was short and brushed back. She smiled.

"Excuse my defensiveness," she said.

Jesse nodded.

"I understand you are going to bring in a few kids this summer, to get them started."

She nodded.

"Yes," she said. "A kind of pilot program."

"And later add some more kids?"

"When the school year starts and if things have gone well, maybe."

Jesse nodded.

"Your constituency," she said, "probably has used the camel's-nose-in-the-tent phrase by now."

"They have," Jesse said.

"And traffic," Nina Pinero said.

She was dressed in white pants and a black sleeveless top. Her clothes fit her well.

"That, too," Jesse said.

"You believe them?"

"No. They are fearful that when it's time to sell their home, the prospective buyers will be discouraged by a school full of Hispanic Americans."

"They have, I know, already tried the zoning route," Nina Pinero said.

"Town council tells me there are no zoning limits in Paradise that apply to schools," Jesse said. "There are regulations about what you can put near a school but none about what you can put a school near."

"That's right."

"You've done your homework," Jesse said.

"Yes."

"You have legal advice?"

"I'm a lawyer," she said.

"And yet so young and pretty," Jesse said.

"My only excuse is that I don't make any money at it," she said.

Jesse nodded.

"How old are these kids?" Jesse said.

"Four, five, a couple are six."

"Best and the brightest?" Jesse said.

"Yes."

"How do they feel about breaking trail?" he said.

"Scared," she said.

"But willing?"

"Marshport," Nina Pinero said, "is not a good place to be a kid. Most of them are scared anyway. This way maybe we can save a few of them."

"Not all of them?"

"God, no," Nina Pinero said. "Not even very many of them. But it's better than saving none."

"Sort of like being a cop," Jesse said.

"You do what you can," she said.

They sat quietly for a moment. The room was not air-conditioned, and the windows were open. Jesse could hear the thump of the basketball on the asphalt court.

"You're making your initial run Monday?" Jesse said.

"Yes. Do you expect trouble?"

"Probably not. Do you think the kids would mind if I rode the bus with them?"

"You?"

"Me and one of my officers," Jesse said. "Molly Crane. I'd wear my uniform and polish up my badge."

"You do think there might be trouble."

"Not really," Jesse said. "But there could

be a picket or two. I'm thinking about the kids mostly."

"Reassured by your presence?"

"Yes. And Molly's."

"Mostly, they are afraid of policemen," Nina Pinero said.

"Maybe Molly and I can help them get past that," Jesse said.

Nina Pinero nodded thoughtfully.

"Yes," she said. "I can see how you might."

12.

In the Gray Gull, Crow was nursing Johnnie Walker Blue on the rocks at the bar when his cell phone rang. He checked the caller ID, and answered it as he walked outside to talk.

"The kid charged a big television set," a voice said at the other end.

"On your account?" Crow said.

"Yeah. She got one of those satellite cards, you know? Her name's on it, but the bill comes to me."

"Her real name?"

"Yeah."

"She know the bill comes to you?" Crow said.

"Who knows what she knows. Bills been coming to me all her life. I doubt that she ever thought about who pays. Hell, she may not even know that somebody has to."

Crow smiled in the darkness outside the Gray Gull.

"Where'd she get it," Crow said.

"Place called Images in Marshport, Massachusetts."

"So she is around here," Crow said.

"I told you she would be."

"What kind of TV?" Crow said.

"I wrote it down," the voice said.

It was a soft voice. But there was tension in it, as if it wanted to yell and was being restrained.

"Mitsubishi 517," the voice said. "Fifty-five-inch screen."

"So she didn't carry it away," Crow said.

"Not her," the voice said.

"Maybe they'll tell me where they sent it," Crow said.

"Maybe," the voice said.

The connection broke. Crow folded up his cell phone and put it away. He stood for a moment looking across the parking space toward the harbor.

"When I find her," he said aloud, "then what?"

13.

The small bus was yellow, with school-bus plates. And the usual signage about stopping when the lights were flashing. The driver was a white-haired Hispanic man who spoke too little English to have a conversation. Jesse stood in the exit well beside the driver. Molly sat in back with Nina Pinero. Both Molly and Jesse were in full uniform. Jesse even had on the town-issued chief's hat with braid on the front. The children's clothes were spruced and ironed. The children themselves were very quiet. Jesse could see them swallowing nervously. Several of them kept clearing their throats. And though most of them were dark-skinned, Jesse could see that their faces were pale.

The bus went past Paradise Beach. No one paid any attention. The kids looked at the hot-dog stand. The bus moved out onto the causeway with the crowded harbor to the left and the open Atlantic to the right. The kids stared out the window. The silence in the bus was palpable. Jesse made no attempt to reassure the kids. He knew how useless that was. Across the causeway, the bus went straight ahead on Sea Street. Past the Paradise Yacht Club. The bus stopped in front of a fieldstone wall that separated a rolling lawn from the street. Across the street there was a white van with a big antenna. On the side it said action news 3. At the top of the lawn was a huge weathered-shingle house. A wide, white driveway wound from behind the house down across the big lawn to the opening in the stone wall, where it joined the street. In the opening, on the driveway, there were maybe twenty adults in varying hues of seer-sucker and flowered hats. Among them in an on-air summer dress and a big glamorous hat was Jenn. With her was a cameraman in a safari vest.

Nina Pinero stood and walked down to the front of the bus. Molly stayed in the rear. She stopped beside Jesse. Jesse nodded at the driver and he opened the bus doors. Jesse stepped out. The gathered adults stared at him. Walter Carr stood with Miriam Fiedler. They both had pamphlets ready. Jesse wondered who they planned to hand them out to.

"Hello," Jesse said. "I've come to protect you from the invaders."

Carr said, "What?"

"I'm here, with Officer Crane, to see that not one of these small savages attacks you or in any way harms your property," Jesse said.

"There's no need to be caustic, Chief Stone," Miriam Fiedler said. "We are simply trying to maintain the integrity of our property and the safety of our streets."

Jesse nodded at Nina Pinero, and she gently pushed a little boy forward. Jesse took his hand as he stepped from the bus.

"Meet the enemy," Jesse said.

The boy was wearing sandals and khaki shorts, and a snow-white T-shirt. Jesse could feel the stiffness in his hand when he held it.

"His name," Jesse said, "is Roberto Valdez. He was five last week."

Nina gently directed a little girl from the bus. Jesse took her hand as she stepped down. She had on red sneakers with red-and-white striped laces, and white shorts and a white T-shirt.

"This is Isabel Gomez," Jesse said. "She won't be five until later this month."

He could feel Isabel tremble a little as he held her hand.

"Okay, Isabel," Jesse said. "You stand with Roberto, right here, beside the bus, behind me."

"Is this really necessary, Chief Stone?" Miriam Fiedler said.

"Yes, ma'am," Jesse said. "It is."

One by one, the kids emerged from the bus and stood fearfully with Jesse for a moment while he introduced them. Finally they were through. Molly got out of the bus and stood with the kids. Nina Pinero got out and stood beside Jesse.

"Chief Stone," Austin Carr said, "we do not have any animosity toward these children. We would support them, and I mean financially, if they wished to establish a nice school and summer camp in Marshport."

At the top of the driveway, several young

men and women in shorts and T-shirts came out of the house and stood, waiting.

"Staff is in place," Nina Pinero said to Jesse.

"Okay," Jesse said. "Follow me, kids."

"This is outrageous," Miriam Fiedler said. "We are not a bunch of rabble to be brushed aside."

"You're not?" Jesse said.

With Nina Pinero and Molly herding the children behind him, Jesse walked straight through the seersucker circle and up the driveway. Behind him he heard Miriam Fiedler cry out in pain.

He heard Molly say, "Oh, dear, I'm so sorry. I seem to have stepped on your foot."

Jesse didn't turn around to look. But he smiled as he led the kids up the driveway.

14.

Wilson Cromartie, in a tan summer suit and a yellow gingham shirt, walked down the center passage of a big mall that had replaced the nineteenth-century brick buildings in the heart of Marshport. There were some shoppers, but the majority of the people in the mall were Hispanic teenagers, in the various costumes of their age group. A number of them were in a store called Images, gazing at the television sets they couldn't afford.

Crow went into the store.

"My daughter bought a big-screen TV here a while ago," Crow said to the clerk. "And the delivery seems to have gone astray."

"Astray?"

"Yes," Crow said. "She never got it."

"Oh, my," the clerk said.

He turned to the computer.

"What's your daughter's name, sir?"

"Amber Francisco," Crow said.

The clerk worked the computer for a moment.

"Twelve-A Horn Street?" the clerk said.

Crow nodded. The clerk smiled.

"It was delivered ten days ago," the clerk said. He was triumphant. "Signed for by Esteban Carty."

Crow looked puzzled.

"Here in Marshport?"

"Yes, sir. If you'd like to step around the counter, I can show you."

"No," Crow said. "Thank you. That'll be fine."

He shook his head.

"Damn kid will put me in an early grave," he said.

He left the store. As he walked back through the mall, several of the teenage girls lounging about watched him as he passed.

15.

Jenn came into the police station with her cameraman, waved at Molly, and came to Jesse's office, the cameraman behind her.

"No cameras in the station," Jesse said when he saw them.

The cameraman looked at Jenn.

"You want to make it a freedom-of-the-press thing?" he said.

Jenn grinned.

"Go ahead, Mike," Jenn said. "Take a break in the van. I'll just talk with Jesse."

The cameraman picked up his camera and went out. Jenn sat across from Jesse.

"Very impressive," she said.

Jesse nodded.

"Riding in with the little kids. Introducing them. Made the protesters look foolish," Jenn said.

Jesse nodded again.

"I kind of liked it also," Jenn said, "when Molly stomped on that woman's foot."

"Molly being Molly," Jesse said.

"I am woman, hear me roar," Jenn said.

"I suspect Molly would be Molly with or without feminism," Jesse said.

Jenn nodded.

"I like her," Jenn said.

"I like her, too," Jesse said.

"What do you suppose the protesters really want in all of this?" Jenn said.

"We on the record here, Jenn?"

"I'd like to be," Jenn said.

Jesse nodded.

"No comment," he said.

Jenn leaned back a little in her chair and looked at Jesse with her head tilted to the side. Her summer dress had slid up to mid-thigh. Her legs were tan. Jesse felt the feeling. He had felt the feeling for such a long time now that it was nearly routine. Sometimes he thought it was the only feeling he had.

"Okay, then," Jenn said. "Off the record."

"First, a question for you," Jesse said. "How'd you happen to be there."

"It's news," Jenn said with a smile. "A lawyer named Blake called us up and informed us of that."

Jesse shook his head.

"They actually think if they get coverage," Jenn said, "they'll get sympathy."

Jesse nodded.

"Maybe a little out of touch," Jesse said. "They probably have a couple of problems with the Crowne estate project. Neither of which, as you may have observed, is traffic."

"Hell," Jenn said. "Our van took up as much space as your bus."

"It did," Jesse said. "One of their problems is they fear a decrease in the value of real estate around the school. And if everybody is like them, the real estate next to a school for disadvantaged children will be harder to sell. And they think that everybody is like them. Or at least everybody who counts."

"They do seem insular," Jenn said.

"Most people are."

"What's their other problem?" Jenn said.

"They don't want a bunch of low-class wetbacks moving into Paradise."

"Simple bigotry?" Jenn said.

"It's almost always that," Jesse said, "when you wipe away the bullshit."

"Wow," Jenn said. "Cynical, cynical, cynical."

"I like to think of it as profiting from the learning experience," Jesse said.

"May I use any of this?"

"No."

"Why not?"

"Because it was off the record," Jesse said. "Feel free to use anything I said on the record."

"The only thing you said on the record was 'no comment.'"

"Feel free," Jesse said.

16.

Mostly Molly ran the front of the police station, but she had persuaded Jesse to allow her, at least once a week, to take a shift on patrol. Jesse had not wanted her shift to be at night. But after Molly explained that he was treating her like a woman, not a cop, and that she was both and should be treated as both, Jesse put her out every couple of weeks, at night, in one of the two patrol cars.

Tonight she was cruising Paradise Neck. She liked the night patrol. Every night would be awful. She'd never see her husband or her kids. But once every couple of weeks it was very soothing. She felt safe enough. Paradise was hardly a war zone. She also had a .40-caliber handgun, Mace, a nightstick, a radio, and the shotgun locked to the dashboard.

She smiled. *Armed to the teeth.*

She passed a pickup truck parked on Ocean Street. *White-collar affectation,* she thought. Riding in the soft darkness, she could think about things like white-collar affectation. She could worry about her children. She could ponder what would become of them. She could think about her husband and herself when the kids had grown. She giggled to herself. She could think about Wilson Cromartie, known as Crow. She shook her head. She had never cheated on her husband. Probably never would. If she did, it would probably be with Jesse, and not an Apache gunman. And even if she wanted to cheat with Jesse, she was not sure he'd allow it. He had so many little rules. *Which,* she said to herself, *is one of the reasons you find him attractive in the first place.*

As she rounded a curve on Ocean Street she saw dimly a man coming down the front walk of one of the big houses that overlooked the Atlantic on the outer side of the Neck. It was 3:10 in the morning. She slowed when she saw him. He paused in the shadow of a shrub and waited. She drove slowly past. Around the next bend she U-turned and drove back. The man was walking back down Ocean Street toward where she'd seen the pickup truck. He was a big man, and his walk looked familiar. She pulled up beside him and looked. Then she pulled ahead and parked and lowered her window.

"Suitcase Simpson," she said. "You get right in this cruiser, right now."

Suitcase said, "Hi, Molly," and got in beside her.

"That your truck up ahead?" Molly said.

"Yep."

"Was that Miriam Fiedler's house you were coming out of when I passed you before and you tried to hide in the bushes?"

"I wasn't hiding," Suitcase said.

"You were, too, and it is Miriam Fiedler's house," Molly said.

Suitcase shrugged.

"You doing some off-duty security work?" Molly said.

Suitcase looked at her and grinned.

"No," he said. "I was banging Mrs. Fiedler."

"Suit," Molly said, "you dog."

Suitcase smiled and nodded.

"Where's Mr. Fiedler?"

"He travels," Suit said, "a lot."

"Weren't you, in your elegant phrase, banging Hasty Hathaway's wife a few years back?"

"I was," Suit said.

"And not embarrassed about it," Molly said.

"She was hot," Suit said.

"And Mrs. Fiedler?" Molly said. "With the teeth?"

"You'd be surprised," Suit said.

"You together often?" Molly said.

"Whenever Mister goes traveling."

"Which is often."

"Often enough," Suitcase said.

"You think there's any conflict of interest here?" Molly said. "We're sort of opposing her efforts to keep the Latinos out of the Crowne estate."

"Sleeping with the enemy?" Suit said.

"You might say that," Molly said.

"We don't talk about the Crowne estate when we're together."

"What do you talk about?"

"Sex stuff," Suit said.

"Jesus," Molly said.

She stopped the cruiser beside Suit's truck.

"You want to hear what she says when we're in bed together?" Suit said.

"Good God, no," Molly said. "I'm already horrified."

"It'll be our secret, though, right, Moll?" Suit said. "Chief might not like it."

"He's nobody to disapprove," she said. "I'm surrounded by a bunch of billy goats."

Suit got out of the cruiser. He leaned his head back in through the open door.

"Mum's the word, Moll?" he said

"Mum," Molly said.

Suit closed the door and got in his truck.

As she drove away, Molly giggled.

"Miriam Fiedler," she said aloud. "Oh, my sweet Jesus."

17.

The sun shining through the window made a long, bright splash on the far wall of Dix's office. Dix was at his desk. As always, he was immaculate. His white shirt gleamed. His bald head shone. The crease in his gray slacks could have been used to sharpen pencils. His cordovan loafers gleamed darkly.

"Why do you suppose she's like that?" Jesse said to Dix.

"Sounds as if her career matters to her," Dix said.

"More than I do," Jesse said.

Dix shrugged.

"She's still pursuing the career," he said.

"And not me," Jesse said.

"Is that true?" Dix said.

"No," Jesse said. "She does still pursue me."

Dix nodded. The air-conditioning made its quiet sound.

"Maybe she wants both," Dix said.

"I don't see why they'd be mutually exclusive," Jesse said.

Dix was quiet. It was always amazing to Jesse how still Dix could be, and yet how clearly his stillness could speak. Jesse knew that in the language of psychotherapy, Dix was asking him to examine that issue.

"Do you?" Jesse said.

"I only know what you tell me," Dix said.

"The hell you do," Jesse said.

"I only know about you and about Jenn by listening to what you tell me about you and about Jenn."

"And bringing to bear thirty years of training and experience to interpret what you heard," Jesse said.

Dix smiled and tipped his head in acceptance.

"We won't divert ourselves with the difference between knowing and interpreting," Dix said. "Let's just agree that my innocence is a fiction that is useful to the process."

"Okay," Jesse said. "What you know, if you're a cop, is that what people say needs to be compared to what they do."

Dix seemed to nod.

"So," Jesse said, "Jenn left me to pursue her career but never quite let go, and has ricocheted between me and her career ever since."

"What do you suppose her career represents to her?" Dix said.

"Represents?"

Dix again almost nodded.

"Sometimes," Jesse said, "a cigar is just a cigar."

Dix smiled.

"And sometimes it's not," Dix said.

They were quiet. The sunsplash on the wall had become longer.

"She started out trying to be an actress," Jesse said, "and kind of morphed into a weather girl."

"In California?" Dix said.

"No," Jesse said. "Here."

Dix nodded.

"I assume she came here because I was here," Jesse said.

Dix nodded again.

"And then she morphed into a soft-feature reporter," Jesse said. "She did a special on Race Week, few years ago."

Dix waited.

"And then she sort of morphed into an investigative reporter when we had the big murder case last year."

"Walton Weeks," Dix said. "National news. How'd she draw that assignment?"

"Probably because she was my ex-wife," Jesse said. "They figured it would give her access."

"Did it?"

"Some," Jesse said.

Dix waited.

"So I'm kind of tangled up in her career," Jesse said.

Dix waited.

"And sometimes she exploits me," Jesse said.

Dix didn't move.

"And sometimes," Jesse said, "it's like she compromises her career because of me."

Dix made no sign. Jesse didn't say anything else for a while.

Then he said, "So her career and me are clearly tied together in some way."

Dix looked interested. Jesse was silent again. Then he looked at Dix and spread his hands.

"So what?" he said. "I don't know where to go with it."

Dix was quiet for a long time. Then he apparently decided to prime the pump.

"What's your career mean to you?" Dix said.

"Redemption," Jesse said. "We already settled that in here."

"Uh-huh."

"Redemption for being a drunk and a lousy husband..." Jesse said.

"And for getting hurt," Dix said, "and washing out of baseball?"

"Yeah, that, too."

"Being a good cop is your chance," Dix said.

"To be good at something," Jesse said. "I know, we already talked about that."

They were quiet again. Jesse had done this long enough to know that the fifty minutes were almost up.

"You think her career is her chance at redemption?" Jesse said.

"I don't know," Dix said. "What do you think?"

"Weather girl isn't much of a redemption," Jesse said.

"How about investigative reporter?"

Jesse nodded.

"I just demeaned her a little, didn't I," he said.

Dix didn't answer.

"I must be madder at her than I know," Jesse said.

"Almost certainly," Dix said.

"You think she's after redemption?" Jesse said.

Dix looked at his watch, as he always did before closing the session.

"We'll have time to think about that on our own," Dix said. "Until next time. Time's up for today."

"Hell," Jesse said. "Just when it was getting good."

18.

Crow stood in front of a three-decker on an unpaved street that was little more than old wheel ruts overgrown with stiff, gray-green weeds. There were tenements on either side of the rutted street, the paint long peeled, the clapboards gray and warped with weather. A street sign nailed to one of the tenements read horn street. Crow walked down to a sagging three-decker that blocked the end of the street. Over the skewed front door was a number 12.

A small path that might once have been a driveway ran around the tenement and Crow followed it, walking carefully to avoid the beer cans, fast-food cartons, dog droppings, used condoms, discarded tires, bottles, rusted bicycle parts, and odd bits of clothing and bedding that were strewn outside the building. Behind the tenement was a metal garage, which had been repainted without being scraped. The bright yellow finish was lumpy and uneven. The maroon trim, Crow noticed, had been applied freehand and not very precisely. A window in the side of the garage had a window box haphazardly affixed below it. The box was filled with artificial flowers. The garage door was ajar. Above the garage door was the number 12A.

Crow went through the half-open door into the garage.

Inside, there were six young men and a huge rear-projection television set. The young men were drinking beer and watching a soap opera. When Crow stepped into the garage they all came to their feet.

"Who the fuck are you," one of them said.

"I'm looking for Esteban Carty," Crow said.

"And I said who the fuck are you?"

"My name is Wilson Cromartie," Crow said. "You Carty?"

"You ain't a cop."

The speaker was short, with shoulder-length black hair and a full beard. He was wearing a tank top and there were gang tattoos up each arm.

"Cops don't come in here alone," he said.

"I'm still looking for Esteban Carty," Crow said. "And I'm getting tired of asking."

"Hey, Puerco," the long-haired kid said. "Wilson getting tired of asking."

Puerco was big, with a shaved head, weight-lifter muscles, no shirt, and a round, hard belly. His upper body was covered with tattoos, including one across his forehead: PUERCO.

Puerco stared at Crow. He had very small eyes for so large a man. There was something else peculiar about his eyes, Crow thought. Then he realized that Puerco had no eyebrows. Crow wondered if it was a defect of nature, or if Puerco had shaved them so as to look more baleful.

"Getting tired of Wilson," Puerco said.

"People do," Crow said.

"Throw him the fuck out," the long-haired kid said.

"*Sí,* Esteban," Puerco said.

"Okay," Crow said, "you're Carty. I'm looking for Amber Francisco."

Puerco stepped across the room toward Crow. Without appearing even to look at him, Crow hit him with the edge of his right hand on the upper lip directly below the nose. Puerco screamed. It was so explosive that none of the others had time to react before Crow had a gun out and pointed at them. Puerco went down, doubled up on the floor, his face buried in his hands, moaning.

"So," Crow said. "Where do I find Amber Francisco."

"I don't know nobody named Amber Francisco," Carty said.

"Girl who bought you the television," Crow said. "What's her name?"

"No bitch bought me nothing," Carty said.

Crow lowered the gun and shot Puerco through the head as he lay moaning on the floor.

Esteban Carty said, "Jesus."

No one else spoke or moved. Crow pointed the gun at Esteban Carty.

"Amber Francisco?" Crow said.

"Bitch bought me the TV name is Alice," Esteban said, "Alice Franklin."

"Where's she live?" Crow said.

"She lives in Paradise, man, her and her old lady."

"Thank you," Crow said. "I'll kill anybody comes out this door while I'm in sight."

Then he stepped through the door and walked away through the trash, toward the street.

19.

Molly came into Jesse's office with Miriam Fiedler right behind her. Molly stopped in the doorway, blocking Miriam Fiedler from entering.

Molly said, "Ms. Fiedler to see you, Jesse."

There was a glitter of amusement in Molly's eyes.

"Show her in," Jesse said. "You stay, too."

Molly stepped aside and Miriam Fiedler brushed past her angrily.

"This woman is deliberately annoying," she said.

"I doubt that it's deliberate," Jesse said. "Probably can't help it. Probably genetic."

"I find her impertinent," Miriam Fiedler said.

"Me, too," Jesse said.

Molly sat down to the right of Miriam Fiedler and behind her.

"Is she going to stay here during our meeting?" Miriam said.

"Yes," Jesse said.

"I don't want her here," Miriam said.

Jesse nodded. Miriam waited. Jesse didn't speak.

"Are you going to send her out?" Miriam said.

"No," Jesse said.

"Chief Stone," Miriam said, "may I remind you that I am a resident of this town, and as such am, in fact, your employer?"

"You may remind me of that," Jesse said.

"Are you being sarcastic?" Miriam said.

"Yes," Jesse said.

"I find it offensive," Miriam said.

"Ms. Fiedler," Jesse said, "it is standard practice in this office that Officer Crane be present when a woman is alone with any male police officers. She will stay as long as you are here."

"Well, it's a stupid rule," Miriam said.

"Did you come to berate me?" Jesse said. "Or have you something substantive?"

"I wish to report several instances of Hispanic gang infiltration of Paradise," she said. "Ever since that school was established on Paradise Neck..."

Jesse nodded.

"Specifically?" he said.

"Specifically," Miriam said, "I have recently seen several Hispanic gang members on the street in downtown Paradise."

"How recently," Jesse said.

"In the last two days."

"And how did you know they were Hispanic gang members."

"Well, my dear man," Miriam said, "you can tell just looking."

"What did they look like?" Jesse said.

"Dark, tattoos, one of them was wearing some sort of hairnet."

"Dead giveaway," Jesse said. "How many did you see."

"Two one day," Miriam said. "And three yesterday, walking side by side, so that they took up the whole sidewalk."

"Did they do anything illegal?" Jesse said.

"Well, they weren't here to sightsee," Miriam said.

"But you are not actually reporting a crime?" Jesse said.

"The press is investigating this, too," Miriam said.

"I heard," Jesse said. "Have they uncovered a crime?"

"Take that attitude if you wish," Miriam said. "When they hurt someone, then you'll act?"

"We'll keep an eye out," Jesse said.

"Maybe you can put Officer Simpson on the case," Molly said. "Any assignment he has, he's on top of it."

Miriam Fiedler turned her head involuntarily to stare at Molly. Jesse saw it. He glanced at Molly. She was smiling sweetly at Miriam Fiedler. Jesse decided to look into the remark later.

"I am not empowered by law to run someone out of town," Jesse said. "I wish I were. But we'll be on the lookout."

"Those children," Miriam said. "They are the camel's nose under the tent."

"And it's a slippery slope from there, I imagine," Jesse said.

"Perhaps I should take my story to the media," Miriam said.

"Perhaps you already have," Jesse said.

"I beg your pardon?"

Jesse waved his hand.

"Well, whether I have or not," Miriam said,

"I certainly shall. And I expect a more sympathetic hearing than I get from you."

"They are permitted to deal in allegation and innuendo," Jesse said. "I am not."

"I know what I saw," Miriam said.

"We both do," Jesse said. "Molly, could you show Ms. Fiedler out, please."

20.

Crow sat in his rental car parked on a curb in the old town section of Paradise, where the houses crowded against the sidewalk. He had circled the block for more than an hour before a spot had opened up within view of the narrow old house on Sewall Street where Mrs. Franklin lived with her daughter. He sipped some coffee from a big paper cup. He wasn't impatient. He had all the time necessary. No hurry. Crow couldn't really remember ever being in a hurry.

A little after two in the afternoon, a big woman with a lot of coal-black hair came out of the house and started up the street. Her hair was a black that no Caucasian woman could achieve without chemical help. She probably wasn't quite as heavy as she looked, but her breasts were so ponderous that they enlarged her. She wore large harlequin sunglasses.

Crow took a photograph from his inside pocket and looked at it and then at the woman. *Could be.* She passed the car barely three feet from Crow. Up close, her face was puffy and reddish. She wore too much makeup, badly applied. She would be older now, and, of course, the picture was a glamour shot, designed to make her look as good as she could. She was blonde in the picture. But that was easily changed. *Probably her.*

Crow made no move to follow her. He simply sat. In about twenty minutes she came back carrying a paper bag. As she passed the car, Crow could see that the bag contained two six-packs of beer. She went back into her house and closed the door behind her. Crow sat. At about 3:50 the front door opened again and a girl came out. She, too, had very black hair. But hers had a candy-apple-red stripe in it. She used black lipstick and a lot of black makeup around her eyes. She had on a mesh tank top and cutoff denim shorts and black cowboy boots with a red dragon worked into the leather.

Crow took out another picture and looked at it. It was a school picture taken several years ago. Again, the hair color had changed. The makeup was different. She was older. But it was probably Amber Francisco, aka Alice Franklin. She passed Crow heading in the same direction as her mother had, toward Paradise Square. After she passed, he watched her in the rearview mirror. At the top of Sewall Street she met three kids on the corner. They were three of the survivors from 12A Horn Street. One of them was Esteban Carty. The girl and the three men went around the corner. Crow tapped "shave and a haircut, two bits" on the tops of his thighs for a moment. Then he took a cell phone out of the center console and punched up a number.

"I found her," he said. "Her and her mother. But in a couple minutes she's going to know I found her. How you want me to handle it."

"How's she look," the voice said at the other end of the connection.

"The kid?" Crow said.

"Of course the kid, I don't give a fuck how Fiona looks."

Crow smiled but kept the smile out of his voice.

"Looks fine," he said.

"She pretty?"

"Sure," Crow said.

"She's fourteen now, sometimes they change."

"She looks great," Crow said.

"Fiona know about you?"

"Not yet. I assume the kid will tell her," Crow said.

"She might. She might not. Can't take the chance. Kill Fiona and bring me the kid."

Crow took the cell phone from his ear for a moment and looked at it. Then he put it back and spoke into it.

"Sure," he said, and folded shut his cell phone and sat where he was.

21.

"You guys reestablish contact with Crow yet?" Jesse said.

He was in the squad room with Suitcase Simpson, Arthur Angstrom, Peter Perkins, and Molly.

"He knows he's being tailed," Suit said. "He loses us whenever he wants to. You know that."

"I know," Jesse said. "Just asking."

"We been staking out his house," Arthur said. "Figure he'll show up there pretty soon."

"Got a notice out on his car?" Jesse said.

"Car's at the house," Arthur said.

"Maybe he's got another one," Jesse said.

"Another one?"

"Leave the car at home," Jesse said. "Take a cab, rent another car. Cops don't have your number."

"If he can spend that kind of dough," Angstrom said.

Arthur was defensive by nature.

"Arthur," Molly said. "This guy left here ten years ago with about twenty million dollars in cash."

"He's got that kind of dough, why's he here working?" Angstrom said.

"Maybe likes the work," Suit said.

"Maybe he owes a guy a favor," Perkins said.

"Maybe he blew the twenty million," Angstrom said.

Jesse shook his head.

"No," he said. "Crow didn't blow the twenty million."

"How do you know," Arthur said.

"He wouldn't," Jesse said. "Why don't you call around to some local rental agencies, see if he rented a car."

"Maybe he didn't use his real name," Arthur said. "Maybe got himself a whole phony ID."

"Maybe," Jesse said.

"But you want me to call."

"I do," Jesse said.

He looked around the squad room.

"Anything else?"

"You still want a cruiser at the Crowne estate when the buses arrive," Molly said.

"Yep."

"Arrival and pickup?"

"Yep."

"That'd be you this morning, Peter," Molly said.

Perkins nodded.

"Anything else?" Jesse said.

No one spoke.

"Okay," Jesse said. "Go to work."

The cops got up and started out.

"Moll," Jesse said. "Could you stick here a minute?"

Molly sat back down.

When the others had left, Jesse said, "Something going on with Suit and Miriam Fiedler?"

"No," Molly said. "Why?"

"The little joke about Officer Simpson being on top of things."

"I was just teasing her," Molly said. "You know I can't stand her."

"Who can," Jesse said.

Molly didn't say anything. Jesse leaned back and stretched his neck a little, looking up at the ceiling.

"I think there's more, Moll," he said after a time.

"More what?"

"I think there's something between Suit and Miriam Fiedler," Jesse said, "that you have probably promised Suit not to tell me about."

"Honestly, Jesse..." Molly said.

Jesse put up a hand as if he were stopping traffic.

"I don't want to put you in the position where you have to break a promise or lie to me. I like you too much. Hell, I depend on you too much."

"Jesse, I..."

Again, Jesse stopped her.

"Suit is very appealing to a certain kind of older, affluent, dissatisfied woman," Jesse said. "They see him as both masculine and cute. Like a big, friendly bear, and he is often in marked contrast to their husbands."

"Like Hasty Hathaway's wife," Molly said.

"Yeah," Jesse said. "Like her. In return, Suit is flattered by the attention of such a woman, and their age and status seem not to be a detriment but an attraction."

"Oedipus again?" Molly said. "Maybe you've been seeing that shrink too long, Jesse."

"In fact," Jesse said, "not long enough. But for whatever reason, Suit has a track record of bopping some surprising women."

"Lot of that going around," Molly said.

Jesse grinned.

"You bet," Jesse said. "And I'm all for it. As long as it does not compromise what we do here."

"You think Suit is doing the hokey-pokey with Miriam Fiedler?" Molly said.

"I do," Jesse said.

"If you were right, would it harm the department?"

"Not if Suit kept it separate," Jesse said. "Not as long as he continues to serve and protect the kids at the Crowne estate."

"You think he wouldn't?" Molly said.

"No," Jesse said. "I think he will. But I don't want him, or us, embarrassed."

Molly nodded.

"I would," she said, "if he were doing something."

"Good," Jesse said.

They sat together for another moment in silence. Then Jesse looked at Molly and said, "Miriam Fiedler?"

And Molly giggled.

22.

It took a long time for Mrs. Franklin to open the door.

When she did, Crow said, "My name is Wilson Cromartie. I work for a man named Francisco."

She tried to shut the door, but Crow wouldn't let her.

"We need to talk," he said, and forced the door open and went in and closed it behind him.

The woman backed away.

"Don't hurt me," she said.

Her voice was blurred and Crow assumed

she'd drunk most of the beer she'd bought earlier.

"I won't hurt you," Crow said.

"He sent you," she said.

"He did. He wants his daughter back."

"He fucking deserves her," the woman said. "How'd you find us."

"Your daughter used a credit card in her own name."

"Dumb bitch," the woman said.

There was an open can of beer on the coffee table in front of the couch. The woman picked it up and drank some.

"He can have her back," the woman said. "I can't do anything with her. But I'm not going back."

"He doesn't want you back," Crow said.

The woman belched softly.

"Good," she said. "'Cause I ain't going."

"He told me to kill you," Crow said.

The woman backed up a step.

"You said you wasn't going to hurt me," she said.

"I'm not," Crow said. "I don't kill women."

"He know that?"

"No."

"What are you doing here?"

"Your daughter's got a boyfriend?"

The woman finished her beer.

"Everybody's her boyfriend, the little slut. Who's she with now?"

"Kid from Marshport named Esteban Carty," Crow said.

"The fucking gangbanger," the woman said.

"Yep."

"She loves those gangbangers," the woman said. "I think she does it to spite me."

Crow nodded. The woman went to the refrigerator and got another beer. While she had the door open, she counted the number of beer cans left.

"I done everything for her, give up everything. Took her away from him. Run off, risked my life taking her with me, so I wouldn't leave her with him. And she comes here and turns into a fucking slut."

"Your daughter's boyfriend knows I found you," Crow said. "She's with him now. So she'll know, too."

"Yeah?"

"I don't want her running off again."

"You think I can stop her?"

"Doesn't matter," Crow said. "I can."

23.

Jenn sat across from Jesse in the Gray Gull, at the window overlooking the harbor. He was sipping a scotch and soda. Jenn had a mojito.

"You're working," Jesse said.

"Why do you think so?"

"You're on expenses," Jesse said, "or you wouldn't have promised to pay for dinner."

Jenn smiled.

"I missed you," she said. "I wanted to talk. You can pay if you'd rather."

"That's okay," Jesse said.

"Secure in your manhood?"

"Something like that," Jesse said.

"I need a favor."

"Sure."

"We have been all over the gang infiltration story," Jenn said. "And I'm not so sure there is a story."

Jesse nodded.

"We keep getting information from a group called Paradise Preserved about gang activity here. But we can't verify much more than a couple of instances of graffiti."

Jesse nodded.

"Are we being jerked around?" Jenn said.

"You are," Jesse said.

"What do they want?"

"They want the Crowne estate project to fail," Jesse said.

"So they are trying to convince people in Paradise that gang invasion is a collateral result?"

"Something like that," Jesse said.

"I suppose it's better than being opposed to education of the young," Jenn said.

"They've discovered, I think, that intimidating five-year-old kids doesn't look good on TV," Jesse said.

"When we talked about this before, I thought you were being defensive and you thought I was being careerist."

"Neither of us was entirely wrong," Jesse said.

Jesse's first drink had been a very small drink. Jenn still had half of hers. His drinking always bothered her. What would she think if he ordered another one? They were divorced and she was sleeping with other men. How much did he have to lose? He gestured toward the waitress.

"No," Jenn said. "I am a careerist, I guess. My job means a great deal to me. As yours does to you."

"I'm good at it," Jesse said. "If I can keep being good at it, maybe I'll get to be good at other things."

"You're good at a lot of things, Jesse."

"Marriage doesn't seem to be one of them," Jesse said.

Jenn shook her head.

"It takes two," Jenn said. "Not to tango."

Jesse smiled.

"I never said you were perfect," he said.

"The mess we're in," Jenn said, "is a collaborative effort. No one person could have created it alone."

Jesse tried to nurse his second drink.

I'll take a sip, he thought, *and put the glass down. And savor the sip. And talk a little.*

Like Jenn does. And have another sip. No hurry.

"You're sure there's no story, then," Jenn said.

"Not the one you came out here for," Jesse said.

Jenn had started to pick up the menu. She stopped, her hand resting on it.

"But there is a story," she said.

Jesse sipped some scotch and put the glass back down carefully on the table. He let the drink ease down his throat.

"The Crowne estate project might make an interesting feature piece," Jesse said.

"Yes!" Jenn said. "My God, yes! The conflict between privilege and poverty. Between real-estate values and human values. It could become a..." She moved her hands in circles while she searched for a word. "It could become a replica...a...ah...a microcosm of the same kind of conflict between haves and have-nots worldwide."

"Wow!" Jesse said.

"It's great," Jenn said. "I can sell this, I can sell this."

"How 'bout the conflict between you and me," Jesse said.

"I haven't quit on that," Jenn said.

"Me either," Jesse said.

Jenn picked up his hand in both of hers and looked at his face.

"I have always loved you," she said. "I love you now."

Jesse smiled.

"But right now you have a story to sell," he said.

"Yes, I do," Jenn said. "And don't dismiss it, Jesse, it might be my way back."

"To what?" Jesse said.

"To you, for crissake, don't you see that? To you."

24.

The woman was on the couch with a half-drunk can of beer on the coffee table in front of her. Her head was tilted back against the top of the couch. Her mouth had fallen open. She was snoring gently. Crow sat across the room. If someone opened the door, Crow would be out of sight behind it. At 11:07 the daughter arrived.

"Ma," she said, and saw her mother slumped on the couch. "Oh, swell," she said. "Have another beer, Ma."

She closed the door and saw Crow.

"Shit!" she said.

Crow smiled at her.

"Should I come back later?" the daughter said. "Or did you fuck her already."

"No need to come back later," Crow said.

The woman on the couch came awake with a startle.

"Alice?"

"I think Daddy's found us," Alice said. "Esteban told me a guy..."

She stopped and looked at Crow.

"You're the guy."

"That visited Esteban?"

"Yes."

"I am," Crow said.

"You shot Puerco," Alice said.

"Only once," Crow said.

"Shot?" the mother said.

"Shut up, Ma," Alice said. "He works for Daddy."

Mrs. Franklin frowned, trying to focus.

"He said he wasn't gonna hurt us," she said.

"Whaddya gonna do?" Alice said.

"Your old man asked me to kill your mother and bring you back to him."

"Kill her," Alice said.

"Yeah."

"And bring me back?" Alice said.

"Yeah."

"You gonna do either one?"

Crow shook his head.

"So whaddya gonna do?"

"I don't know," Crow said. "You got any suggestions?"

"Whyn't you go kill Daddy," she said.

Crow nodded.

"And what would you do then?" he said.

"What I'm gonna do anyway. Move in with Esteban."

"Not on your life," her mother said. "I didn't raise you to slut for no spick gangbanger."

"You didn't raise me at all, you fucking drunk," Alice said. "I go where I want. I want to slut it up with Esteban, you got no say."

"Don't you talk to me that way," her mother said, and struggled to get off the couch.

"You calling me a slut," Alice said. "There's a laugh."

"I rescued you from your father, and you talk to me like this?"

"At least I'm not a fat slut," Alice said. "I'm outta here."

She turned and found Crow standing in front of the door.

"Get the fuck out of my way," she said.

Crow slapped her hard across the face and sent her halfway across the room. She fell back onto the couch beside her mother and began to cry with her face buried in her hands.

"Esteban is going to kill you," she said. "He's going to kill you for Puerco, and now, when I tell him, he'll kill you for me, too."

Crow took his cell phone out and punched in a number.

After a moment he said, "Chief Stone? Wilson Cromartie. We got a situation down here on Sewall Street."

25.

Jesse brought Molly with him. They were all together in the living room. Jesse standing by the door. Molly in the opposite corner so Crow wouldn't be able to shoot them both together. Crow sat on a reversed straight chair, his arms folded across the back. Alice's face was red from Crow's slap, and her heavy black eye makeup had run when she cried.

"Can we talk off the record?" Crow said.

"I don't see why we should," Jesse said.

"Guy named Louis Francisco," Crow said. "Lives in Palm Beach. Does business all over South Florida. He's very, very important in

South Florida. Miami, all over. He's married to this woman, calls herself Frances Franklin, but her real name's Fiona. Fiona Francisco. Kid here, looks kind of like Alice Cooper, is his daughter. She goes by Alice Franklin around here. But her real name's Amber Francisco."

Jesse didn't comment. He waited, leaning on the wall, his arms folded across his chest. In the opposite corner, Molly was watching both women as Crow talked.

"One day, about three years ago, in the middle of the afternoon, Mrs. Francisco"— Crow nodded toward her—"and the kid disappear. Francisco's upset. He don't care too much about Fiona. But he wants the kid."

Crow paused for a moment, thinking about what he'd say next. No one else said anything.

"So," Crow said, "think about it. You're Louis Francisco. You don't know where your daughter is. And you don't know who's got her, or so you say. But you not only want her back but you probably want to get her away from her mother, whom you consider a bad influence."

"He should talk," Fiona Francisco said.

No one paid her any attention.

"What do you do?" Crow said. "You probably hire somebody to find her. Now suppose he did, hypothetically, hire somebody. And suppose the guy found them. And he calls Louis and tells him and Louis says kill the mother, bring the girl to me."

"He would say that," Fiona said. "The prick."

"I'm not going back," Amber Francisco said.

"And here's the kicker," Crow said. "This hypothetical guy doesn't want to do it. He doesn't want to kill the mother and he doesn't want to drag the daughter down to Florida."

"Why?" Jesse said.

"Guy's got his reasons," Crow said. "But hypothetically, he's already annoyed the hell out of the members of a Latino gang in Marshport. And Louis won't be too thrilled with this hypothetical guy, who took a lot of dough up front from Louis and is now not doing what he was signed up for."

"So why doesn't our hypothetical friend tuck his hypothetical ass under him and scoot?" Jesse said.

"Probably wouldn't be his style," Crow said.

"And he doesn't quite want to bail on these women," Jesse said.

"Something like that," Crow said. "If he was an actual guy."

Jesse was nodding his head slowly. Crow waited.

"Okay," Jesse said. "I can't stand this hypothetical crap anymore. We're off the record."

"Which means?" Crow said.

"Which means I won't use anything you say against you," Jesse said.

Crow looked at him for a time.

"Good," Crow said.

"So you got Louis Francisco on your ass," Jesse said, "and I assume he has a lot of resources for getting on your ass."

"He does," Crow said. "On the other hand, I got kind of a hard ass."

From across the room, Molly said, "Uh-huh!"

Crow looked at her and grinned.

"And," Jesse said, "you got a Latino gang on your ass for a reason not yet specified."

"Correct."

"And you want me to keep track of these women while you deal with your other problems."

"Correct."

Jesse was quiet for a moment.

Then he said, "What's in this for me?"

"Do the right thing?" Crow said.

Jesse stared at him.

"Crow," Jesse said, "how many people you killed in your life?"

"It's bush to count," Crow said.

"And you think I'll do it because it's the right thing to do?"

"Yeah."

"What makes you so sure."

"It's the way you are," Crow said.

"How the hell do you know the way I am?" Jesse said.

"I know," Crow said.

Again, a pause.

Then Jesse said, "Yeah, you probably do."

26.

"I can't hold them for long," Jesse said.

He and Crow were in his office. The Francisco women, mother and daughter, were in the squad room with Molly and Suitcase Simpson.

"Part of a criminal conspiracy?" Crow said.

"I don't think that statute covers the intended victims," Jesse said.

"At least you could put a cop with them," Crow said.

"Yeah," Jesse said. "I can. And I will. But if either or both decides to run off, my cop can't stop them."

"You got them now," Crow said.

"For questioning. They can leave when they want to."

Crow didn't say anything.

"Why do you care about any of this?" Jesse said.

"Why not?" Crow said.

"Why'd you take the job in the first place? You need the money?"

"Hell, no," Crow said. "I came into a lot of money, 'bout ten years ago."

"So...?"

"Being rich can get boring," Crow said. "I like to work. Francisco leads me to think there might be some push and shove when I found the women. He led me to believe that somebody might be with them that would need to be..." Crow made a small rolling gesture with his right hand. "Removed."

"And that would be your kind of work."

"It would," Crow said. "I'm very good at it."

"So you took the job because you wanted to get into it with somebody?" Jesse said.

Crow shrugged.

"No point being a warrior if you can't find a war," he said.

Jesse stared at him.

"Warrior?" Jesse said.

"I am a full-blooded Apache warrior," Crow said.

Jesse looked at him for a sign that he was joking. There was no sign.

"And warriors don't go to war against women and girls," Jesse said.

"No," Crow said, "they don't."

"That's why you let those women hostages go, ten years ago," Jesse said, "off the boat."

"I like women," Crow said.

"If the money had been on shore with Macklin," Jesse said, "would you still have let them go?"

Crow smiled.

"Can't go back and do it different," Crow said.

Jesse nodded. Crow was silent again.

"So how come you decided to look for the Francisco women here?" Jesse said.

"Francisco said he thought they'd be here."

"He say why?"

"Nope."

"You ask?"

"Nope."

"So how'd you find them?" Jesse said.

"Kid charged a big TV set for her boyfriend on one of those satellite credit cards, you know, bill goes to Daddy. Daddy calls me and I run it down. Thing was too big to carry. It was delivered to a gang house in Marshport."

"So you went there," Jesse said.

"Yep."

"Alone."

"Yep."

"How'd you get them to tell you where she was?"

"I had to shoot one of them," Crow said. "Their bad man, guy named Puerco."

"Pig," Jesse said.

"You speak Spanish?"

"Used to work in L.A.," Jesse said. "Had some time in Boyle Heights. Self-defense?"

"Of course."

"What gang?" Jesse said.

"Never mentioned their name."

"Where were they?" Jesse said.

"Dump at the end of an alley called Horn Street. Twelve-A Horn Street."

"Horn Street Boys," Jesse said.

"You know the gangs in Marshport?"

"Like to keep up," Jesse said.

Molly came into the office.

"The women are asking for a lawyer," she said.

Crow studied her.

"Tell them that they can go after they talk with one more cop," Jesse said.

"Who?"

"Who's on the desk?"

"Peter Perkins," Molly said.

"Okay," Jesse said. "Send Suit out front. Tell Peter to ask them anything he can think of."

"Peter doesn't know the case," Molly said. "He doesn't even know their names."

"Doesn't matter."

"We don't get them a lawyer when they ask, any case we bring into court gets tossed."

"Doesn't matter," Jesse said. "We're not bringing a case against them."

"We're just stalling," Crow said, "until we figure out what to do."

Molly turned and looked straight at Crow.

"We?" Molly said.

Crow smiled at her.

"So to speak," he said.

Molly smiled back, and turned and left. Crow watched her go. Jesse was pretty sure she was swinging her hips more than she normally did.

Jesse said, "What do you want out of all this, Crow?"

"I want these two broads to be okay, and have that be my doing."

"Because?"

"I told you," Crow said, "I like women."

"Or you don't," Jesse said.

"Don't?"

"Because they aren't worthy opponents," Jesse said.

Crow shrugged.

"What do you think of the men in their lives?" Jesse said.

"Don't like them. Don't like Francisco. Don't like the gangbanger."

"Because?"

"Because the gangbanger's a punk," Crow said. "And Francisco is a liar."

"You ever wonder why he hired somebody like you to find his daughter?"

"I figured he might want somebody killed along the way."

"And you were willing."

"I was willing to take his money and see what developed," Crow said. "I'm not willing to kill a couple women."

"For the moment," Jesse said.

Crow shrugged.

"'Course, the daughter could turn out to be some sort of hole card for you," Jesse said.

"Could," Crow said.

"You think the mother would abandon her daughter?" Jesse said.

"They do sometimes," Crow said.

"I know," Jesse said. "But often they don't. Maybe we let them go, what happens. Kid isn't going to leave the boyfriend. Mother isn't going to leave the kid. Boyfriend's not going anywhere. Most gang kids never leave the neighborhood until they go to jail."

"Yeah?"

"So they stay right here while I figure out what to do about a couple things," Jesse said.

"Like what?"

"Like how to help them, and what the hell you're up to."

"What if she moves in with him?" Crow said.

"We know where she is," Jesse said.

"Not much of a life on Horn Street," Crow said.

"Not much of a life on Sewall Street, either," Jesse said.

"There's bad and there's worse," Crow said.

"Won't be forever," Jesse said. "Once I get it figured out, we'll go take her away from Horn Street."

"And if she won't come?" Crow said.

"We make her."

"Man, you are cold," Crow said.

"Keep it in mind," Jesse said.

"How come you're going along with any of this?" Crow said.

"Girl's a mess," Jesse said. "Her old man is in the rackets in South Florida..."

"Her old man *is* the rackets in South Florida," Crow said.

"...and her mother's a drunk," Jesse continued. "Kid needs help. And you seem like you might give her some."

Crow nodded.

"Okay," Crow said.

"Let's be clear," Jesse said. "I don't trust you."

"Be crazy if you did," Crow said.

"I don't believe this is pure concern for the Francisco girls," Jesse said.

Crow shrugged.

"Don't matter too much what you believe," Crow said. "Thing you can trust, though. I keep my word."

Jesse nodded.

"And you keep yours," Crow said.

"You think?"

"I know you, Stone, just like you know me.

We been listening to the same music for a long time."

"And we know all the lyrics?" Jesse said.

"All the ones that matter," Crow said.

27.

Jesse invited Nina Pinero to lunch.

"In Marshport?" she said. "You don't eat lunch in Marshport. I'll come to you."

They met at the Gray Gull. The weather was pleasant, so they sat outside on the little balcony over the water.

"Want a drink?" Jesse said when they were seated.

"No, if I do I'll have to go take a nap, and I haven't got time."

Jesse nodded.

"You have one if you want," Nina said.

"No," Jesse said. "I haven't got time, either."

They ordered iced tea. Nina looked out over the harbor. Across the water, the Paradise Yacht Club was visible.

"Long way from Marshport," she said.

"Pretty far from L.A., too," Jesse said.

"That where you're from?"

"It's where I worked before I came here," Jesse said.

"Cop?"

"Yes."

"Why'd you leave?" Nina said.

"They fired me for drinking."

"Ah," Nina said. "Another good reason not to drink at lunch."

Jesse nodded.

"What do you know about Latino gangs in Marshport," Jesse said.

"A lot. It's part of my job."

"What exactly is your job?" Jesse said.

"Do-gooder," she said. "Like you."

"I just do this for the perks," Jesse said.

"Perks?"

"Yeah, I can park where I want and I get to carry a gun."

Nina smiled.

"That's why you rode the bus with the kids and walked them into school," she said.

"Did you see my gun?" Jesse said.

Nina laughed this time.

"Okay, what do you want to know about the gangs?" she said.

"Just one," Jesse said. "Horn Street."

"Oh, my," Nina said. "The Horn Street Boys. That's Esteban Carty."

"Tell me about them."

"Twelve, fifteen kids, hang out in an abandoned garage down at the end of Horn Street. Actually, small world, one of them has a little brother at the Crowne estate project. Esteban is the, I don't know what to call him exactly, the driving force in the gang, I guess. His enforcer is a man name Puerco. Pig or Hog in English, and the name tells you mostly what you need to know. He is a fearsome psychopath. Even the cops are afraid of Puerco."

Jesse smiled.

"What?" Nina said.

"They don't have to be scared of him anymore," Jesse said.

"Something happened to Puerco?"

"He got killed a few days ago," Jesse said.

"Puerco?"

"Yep."

"God," Nina said, "I'd like to see the man who could kill Puerco."

"Anybody can kill anybody," Jesse said. "It's just a matter of what you're willing to do."

"You ever kill anyone?" Nina said.

"Yes."

They were quiet for a moment.

Then Nina said, "Esteban Carty has been on his own since he was little. I don't know what he had for family. Maybe none, ever. He's like a feral child grown up."

"So he's probably not bound by societal convention," Jesse said.

"Oh, God, no," Nina said. "That's what the gang is for."

"Any thoughts on what kind of boyfriend he'd make for a fourteen-year-old girl?" Jesse said.

She shook her head.

"Outside my purview," she said. "I'm neither a shrink nor a fourteen-year-old girl."

"But you're female and you know something about Esteban," Jesse said. "Puts you two up on me."

"I believe that one of the rules of the Horn

Street Boys is that girlfriends have sex with everyone in the gang," Nina said. "All for one and one for all."

"Great for building camaraderie," Jesse said.

28.

They were naked together on the bare mattress of a rusted daybed against the wall opposite the big-screen TV in the garage at the foot of Horn Street.

"Esteban," Amber said, "what if somebody comes in?"

"Who's gonna come in 'cept Horn Street Boys?" Esteban said.

"But they'll see us."

"Won't be seeing nothing they ain't seen," Esteban said.

"I know," she said. "I'm just kind of not used to doing it like this, you know, like out in the open?"

"You moved in here. You're one of us now," Esteban said, and pressed on.

When it was over, she said, "I bet you've done a lot of girls on this couch."

"A lot," Esteban said.

"Anyone as hot as me?" she said.

"No, no, baby, you're the hottest."

There was no sound of Spanish in his voice. She wished there were. It would be more romantic. She wasn't sure he even spoke Spanish beyond a few phrases.

"So who's this dude, shot Puerco?" Esteban said.

"Wilson Cromartie," she said. "He calls himself Crow and he says he's an Apache Indian."

"I don't give a fuck he's a martian, you know? What's he want with you?"

"My daddy hired him to bring me home."

"Your daddy?"

"Yes," Amber said. "Daddy hired this guy to find me and my old lady, and kill the old lady, and bring me home."

"What's your daddy's name?"

"Louis Francisco," Amber said.

"That your real name?" Esteban said.

"Yes. Amber. Is that a sappy name? Amber Francisco."

"Yeah. Where's Daddy live?"

"Miami," Amber said. "He's very rich."

Esteban nodded.

"What's he do?"

"I don't know. He's in a bunch of businesses."

"You like him?" Esteban said.

"Hell, no," Amber said. "He's in on all kinds of shady shit, you know? And he sends me to the fucking convent school. You know? Nuns. Jesus!"

Esteban nodded.

"And he wants your old lady killed?"

"Yeah."

A couple of Horn Street Boys came into the garage. Amber rolled over onto her stomach. Neither of them paid any attention to her. They got beer from the refrigerator, sat down on a couple of rickety lawn chairs, picked up the remote from the floor, and turned on a soap opera. Amber hated soap operas. Her mother used to watch them in the big, empty house and drink beer until she fell asleep on the couch. Amber wished they'd shut it off. She wished she had her clothes on. She wished things were different.

"I think I should talk to your old man," Esteban said.

29.

Crow was sitting under the small pavilion at Paradise Beach, talking on his cell phone. The day was eighty-five and clear. The tide was in. The ocean covered most of the beach, and the waves rolled in quietly, without animosity.

"I'm not going to kill your wife, Louis," Crow said. "And I'm not going to bring your daughter down to Miami."

"You sonovabitch, Crow," Louis Francisco said at the other end of the connection. "I paid you a lot of money."

"To find them," Crow said. "I found them."

"You want to survive this, Crow, you do what I told you."

"Nope."

"If I have to come up there, by God..."

"Probably ought to," Crow said.

"Then I will," Louis Francisco said. "And I won't be coming alone."

The outrage was gone from his voice, Crow noticed. He seemed calm now. He was doing business he understood.

"I'll be here," Crow said, and turned off the cell phone.

He sat for a time looking at the ocean. He liked the ocean. There were young women on the narrow beach, in small bathing suits. He liked them, too. He stood and walked along the top of the beach and onto the causeway that led to Paradise Neck. He stopped halfway across, leaning on the wall, looking at the ocean, breathing in the clean smell of it. It would take Francisco a couple days to organize his invasion. He wondered what the cop would do with that. Stone was a cop, and this was a small town. But Stone wasn't a small-town cop. It interested Crow, how far Jesse would go. Crow was pretty sure Jesse would stick when it came down to it, that Crow could count on him. And he knew that Jesse's cops were loyal to him. The big kid, Suitcase, looked like he could handle himself. And Crow loved the feisty little female cop.

He turned and rested his back against the seawall and looked in at Paradise Harbor. Might be time to call on Marcy Campbell, too. She was good-looking, and, he was pretty sure, she was ready. He smiled. Women forgave him a lot. He watched the harbormaster's boat moving about among the tall pleasure boats riding their mooring, sails stowed, people having lunch on the afterdeck. He looked at his watch. Maybe he should have lunch. Daisy Dyke's? No, that would be iced tea. At the Gray Gull, he could have a couple of drinks with his lunch and then go home and take a nap. He straightened and flexed his shoulders a little to loosen them, and began to walk back to the beach where his car was parked. He felt really good.

Maybe he was going to have his war.

30.

They were all there in the garage. Twelve Horn Street Boys, plus Esteban Carty. Amber sat on the floor in the corner with her arms wrapped around her knees. Listening while Esteban spoke.

"Okay," he said to the Boys, "we got a contract."

The boys seemed pleased.

"Guy gonna give us ten grand to off a broad in Paradise."

The boys responded.

"Ten grand?"

"A broad?"

"Muthafuck, man, how easy is that?"

"Easy," Esteban said.

One of the boys said something in Spanish.

"Knock it off," Esteban said. "We speak English."

Amber wondered randomly if that was some sort of self-improvement rule, or was it because Esteban didn't speak much Spanish. She shrugged mentally. The Horn Street Boys had a lot of rules.

"And here's a gas," Esteban said. "Guy paying us is Alice's father."

Everyone looked at Amber. She giggled. It was nice that Esteban told them.

"Who's the broad?" one of the boys said.

"Are you ready for this?" Esteban said.

Amber could see he was excited. She felt excited, too. He pointed at her like a referee calling a foul.

"Alice's momma," he said.

Everyone looked at her again. Amber giggled again. One of the boys started clapping, and the others joined in. Amber giggled some more, and hid her face.

"Bye-bye, Momma," Esteban said.

And the boys took up the chant.

"Bye-bye, Momma! Bye-bye, Momma! Bye-bye, Momma."

They clapped in rhythm to it and Amber, sitting on the floor, with her face in her hands and her knees up, began to rock back and forth to the chant. After a while she joined in.

"Bye-bye, Momma! Bye-bye, Momma! Bye-bye, Momma!"

31.

"So," Jesse said. "Where were we?"

"I think you know," Dix said.

"We were wondering aloud...no, I was wondering aloud...what Jenn's career meant to her."

Dix nodded.

"I think my last question was, Do you think her career means redemption to her?"

"That's how I remember it," Dix said.

"And you were about to not answer the question," Jesse said.

Dix smiled.

"I hoped you might have a thought," he said.

"I have things to redeem," Jesse said. "But I guess so does she."

Dix inclined his head.

"She has yet to succeed at a job," Jesse said.

"Or a relationship," Dix said.

"Or a relationship," Jesse said. "We both got an oh-for on relationships."

"Except with each other," Dix said.

"This is a good relationship?" Jesse said.

"It's an enduring one," Dix said.

Jesse stared at him.

"Well," Jesse said. "Yeah, I guess so."

"Why do you think that is?"

Jesse paused.

"Love?" he said.

Dix nodded.

"And why do you think it doesn't work better?" Dix said.

"Because I'm a mess," Jesse said.

Dix shook his head almost imperceptibly.

"I'm not a mess?" Jesse said.

"*Mess* is not a very useful term in my line of work," Dix said. "But it is not unusual for someone in your circumstances to take on all the blame for those circumstances, not out of guilt but because it gives them the power to change it."

"So if it's her fault, there's nothing I can do about it," Jesse said. "And if it's my fault, there is?"

"Again, *fault* is not a term I like to use," Dix said. "But just suppose the near-fatal flaw in your relationship resides with her."

"She's too career-driven," Jesse said.

"I would guess," Dix said, "that her ambition is a symptom, not a condition."

"A symptom of what?" Jesse said.

"She said to you something to the effect that success might be her way back to you."

"Yes," Jesse said.

He felt tense. They were about to see around a corner. He didn't know what he'd see yet, but he'd worked with Dix long enough to know that Dix, however obliquely, would bring him to it.

"But wasn't she with you before she began her career?" Dix said.

"Yes."

"So..."

Dix waited. Jesse sat. After a bit he shook his head.

"Nothing," Jesse said.

Dix whistled silently to himself, as if he were mulling something.

Then he said, "Jesse, you must know you fill a room."

Dix rarely used his first name. Jesse was pleased.

"I'm not that big," he said.

"I'm not talking about physical size," Dix said. "You are a very powerful person."

"For a drunk," Jesse said.

"The alcohol may be a saving grace," Dix said.

"Because?"

"It dilutes your power a little," Dix said. "It must be very difficult to be with someone so powerful unless you yourself have power."

Jesse felt a small click in the center of himself.

"So she has to either increase her own power or decrease mine," Jesse said.

Dix pointed a forefinger at Jesse and dropped his thumb as if pretending to shoot him.

"Bingo!" Dix said.

32.

It was 3:12 in the morning when Jesse pulled up in front of the Crowne estate on Paradise Neck. There was already a small generator in place and a couple of spotlights hooked to it. Two Paradise cruisers were there, and the Paradise Fire Rescue vehicle. Suit stood with Molly in the driveway. Peter Perkins squatted on his heels, taking pictures of a corpse. Jesse got out of the car.

"Mrs. Franklin," Molly said, as Jesse walked toward them. "Amber's mother."

Jesse nodded. He walked to the body and stood looking down. A lot of blood glistened darkly on the smooth, green lawn beneath her head. Perkins looked up when Jesse arrived and rested his camera on his thigh.

"Shot in the back of the head," he said from his crouched position. "Can't tell how many times. Small caliber, I think. No exit wounds."

"State ME been notified?"

"Yeah. On the way."

"Any idea how long?" Jesse said.

"That's the ME's line of work. Blood's dry. Body's kind of stiff."

Jesse nodded.

"Who found the body?" he said.

"Suit," Peter Perkins said.

Jesse turned and stared at Simpson, standing with Molly.

"Murder weapon?" Jesse said.

"Haven't searched yet," Perkins said. "It's not under the body."

Jesse nodded and walked over to Suit and Molly.

"How'd you find the body," Jesse said.

"I was just cruising by and I saw this form. So I stopped, investigated, and there she was."

"Cruising by at, what, two-thirty or so in

the morning?" Jesse said. "You weren't on patrol tonight."

"Not tonight, no," Suit said. "I do that sometimes, though, just get up in the night and ride around, you know, see what I can see."

"Just sort of poking into things," Molly said.

Suit blushed a little. Jesse glanced at Molly. She seemed serene.

"Ever vigilant," Jesse said.

Neither Suit nor Molly said anything.

"Who was supposed to be sitting on Mrs. Franklin, Moll?" Jesse said.

"Buddy."

"He arrive yet?"

Molly pointed at the roadway behind Jesse's car.

"Right now," she said.

"Okay, whyn't you see if you can find a clue or something."

They both nodded. And as Jesse walked toward Buddy Hall's cruiser, parked behind Jesse's car, they both took out flashlights and began to walk the lawn, carefully.

"What happened," Jesse said to Buddy Hall.

"She must have snuck out the back,"

Buddy said. "I'm parked right outside her house all night until I hear the radio call about a body on Paradise Neck. So I call in, and Bobby Martin's working the desk, and he tells me Molly called it in to him, and that it's the Franklin broad. And I said, 'Jesus, she hasn't left the house.' And I call Moll on her cell phone and she says yes it is Franklin and she's been shot and I better get over there. So here I am."

"You check her house?" Jesse said.

"No, I come straight here. Should I have?"

"It's okay," Jesse said. "You help Molly and Suit on the crime scene. I'll go over there."

"Yeah, okay. Jesse, I'm sorry if I fucked up. I didn't think she'd sneak away."

"We'll play it as it lays, Buddy," Jesse said. "Go look for clues... and don't step on any."

Buddy Hall nodded his head very hard and hustled toward the wide lawn that led up to the now-empty school. Jesse followed, looking at the ground, walking carefully until he got to Molly.

"Moll," he said. "You run things here. Make sure everything is gone and cleaned up and no trace before those little kids get here at eight a.m."

"Absolutely," Molly said.

A state car pulled up behind the other cars and parked, and a smallish man got out with a doctor's bag.

"Okay," Jesse said. "The state ME. I want a report as soon as he can get us one."

"I'll tell him," Molly said.

They watched as the ME trudged toward the body.

"Suit's got a girlfriend out here," Jesse said. "Doesn't he?"

Molly nodded.

"And she's, ah, inappropriate, probably married," Jesse said.

"Yes."

"And you discovered him, and he's made you promise not to tell."

"Yes. I gave him my word."

"But you can't resist busting his balls a little."

Molly smiled.

"Could you?" she said.

"Probably not," Jesse said. "One thing, though. If who he's banging becomes any kind of issue to a case, I need to know."

"I understand that, Jesse."

"Okay," Jesse said. "I'll trust your judgment."

"You can," Molly said.

"I know," Jesse said.

He walked back to his car and got in and headed back across the causeway toward Mrs. Franklin's house on Sewall Street.

33.

Now that he had to investigate her murder, Jesse decided to call her by her actual name, Fiona Francisco. In which case he could also think of the daughter as Amber Francisco, and stop messing around with the Franklin-slash-Francisco construct in his head.

He parked in front of her house. There were lights on in the front room. He tried the front door. It was locked. He walked around to the side where a tiny alley squeezed between two buildings. Jesse went down the alley. Behind the house was a tiny brick patio that was at a level lower than the front of the house and was accessed by a door in the basement. The door was open. Jesse looked around the patio. Looming behind it was the back end of another old house. To the left was a small set of stone steps that led up to a driveway at street level. The driveway opened onto a side street that ran perpendicular to Sewall. Jesse looked at it and nodded to himself.

He went in through the open door. He was in a cellar that had been converted, probably in the 1950s from the look of it, into a playroom. Pine-paneled walls, vinyl-tile floors, Celotex tile ceiling. The furnace and electrical panel and hot-water heater were in an alcove. Jesse went up the stairs on the far end and into the living room. It smelled like a tavern. There was a half-full bowl of bright orange cheese puffs on the coffee table in front of the shabby couch. There were four beer cans upright on the coffee table and one on its side. All of them were empty. A pink crocheted coverlet lay half turned back on the couch. Cheese puff detritus speckled the couch and the floor near the couch. The television was on, some sort of infomercial. The kitchen was empty, dirty dishes on the counter. A dirty frying pan on the stove. Jesse opened the refrigerator. Twelve cans of beer, some Velveeta, a loaf of white bread, some peanut butter, and three Diet Cokes. On the counter next to an unwashed coffee cup was a bottle of multivitamins.

That oughta balance everything out, Jesse thought.

He walked through the rest of the small house. The beds were unmade. Dirty laundry lay in piles in both bedrooms. There was a still-sodden towel on the bathroom floor. He went back to the living room and leaned against the front door. To his left was a fireplace that had been cold a long time. Over it was a small mantelpiece, and on the mantel was a school photograph of somebody who probably used to be Amber.

The cellar door had been unlocked. There was no sign of forced entry. It looked as if she had gone down to the cellar and out the back door and up the outside steps to the side street and was gone. *Did she walk? Was there a car? How did she end up out on Paradise Neck? More important, how did she end up dead?* It seemed an odd coincidence that she was found on the lawn of the Crowne estate. *Clearly, she had snuck out. There was no reason to go the way she went except to avoid Buddy Hall in the cruiser out front. Why would she sneak out? If she thought the bad ex-husband was after her, she'd have run to the cop, not away from him... Her daughter... If her daughter called... "Ma, it's Amber, can't talk now, sneak out so the cops don't see you and I'll meet you on Sea Street, behind the house."... Maybe love had failed and she was running from her boyfriend.*

Jesse walked to the fireplace and looked at Amber's picture on the mantel. It was in a cheap cardboard holder. The picture was garishly overcolored, as school pictures often are. The girl in it looked blankly sweet, with soft brown hair and a roundish, unformed face. Jesse looked at it for a while. It told him nothing.

Maybe she wasn't looking for help. Maybe she lured her mother out to be killed... Maybe I been a cop too long... but maybe she did. If she did, who did the killing? Esteban? Why? And why take her to the Crowne estate. Did they kill her there? Kill her elsewhere and dump her there?

Jesse walked once more through the house, hoping it might tell him something. All it said to him was that it was an unpleasant place to live. He went out the front door and closed it behind him and got in his car. *'Course, Horn Street wasn't a week in Acapulco, either.*

He started the car and put it in gear and drove back toward the crime scene. The sky was starting to lighten. It was 4:58 on the dashboard clock. It would be daylight soon. Jesse knew it was too early to speculate. But he also knew it wasn't often that somebody got killed for no reason, or got killed by a perfect stranger. Now and then it happened. Like Son of Sam in New York, or the pair that Jesse had put away a few years ago. But they weren't common.

If a few more dumpy beer-drinking women with adolescent daughters get killed, Jesse thought, *I'll revise my position. But right now it's got something to do with Louis Francisco, and Amber, and maybe Esteban Carty. And maybe something about the Crowne estate.*

Or not.

34.

Amber was sitting cross-legged on the day-bed, smoking a joint, while Esteban talked on his cell phone. They were alone in the garage with the huge television screen. The TV was on but silent. They both liked to smoke a joint and watch TV without sound.

"It'll be in the Boston papers, man, you want to go online and see," Esteban said.

He stood in the doorway with his back to Amber, looking down his alley.

"Yeah, I know you'll pay. I still got the other package to deliver."

Amber watched the shapes move on the silent screen. She knew Esteban was talking to someone, and she could hear the words he said, but the words weren't real. What was real were the endlessly fascinating shapes.

"When I get the dough, I'll ship the package," Esteban said.

Amber took in some smoke and held it for a time before she eased it out. The colors on the huge television were very bright and had a kind of inviting density to them. She'd never realized quite how inviting they were.

"Sure it's a lot, man, but I can't just stick it on a plane, you know? I mean, it's gotta be driven down there. And somebody gotta go along with it, you know? I mean, it ain't gonna want to go at all, man. I gotta see to it that it does."

Amber took another toke. The movement and the colors tended to blend into something. She didn't know what. But it made her feel religious.

"Yeah, man," Esteban said. "You call me when you see the news about Momma. We'll arrange the other delivery."

He shut the cell phone off and came to the couch.

"You believe in God, Esteban?" Amber said.

She offered him her half-smoked joint.

"Sure, baby," Esteban said, "long as he believes in me."

"You believe in the devil?"

"Baby," Esteban said. "I am the devil."

Amber giggled. Esteban took a toke and passed the nearly burned-out roach to Amber. She finished it.

"I like to drink wine when we smoke a joint."

Amber was watching the colors. She didn't move. Esteban gave her a smart slap on the side of her butt.

"You gonna get us some wine?" he said.

Amber stood up.

"You don't have to hit so hard," Amber said.

"Told you, baby, I'm the devil."

She giggled happily and went to the refrigerator, and came back with a jug of white wine. She put out two unmatched water glasses and filled each one with the jug wine. There were four more joints rolled and lying beside a box of kitchen matches on the wooden crate that served as a side table. Esteban drank some wine and lit another joint.

"You talking to my daddy?" Amber said.

"Yeah, we was arranging the payoff for putting Momma down."

"Bye-bye, Momma," Amber said, and giggled.

"Bye-bye," Esteban murmured, and sucked in a big lungful of smoke. As it drifted slowly out of his lungs he murmured again, "Bye-bye."

35.

Jenn came into Jesse's office in the late afternoon.

"You look tired," Jenn said to him.

"Up most of the night," Jesse said. "I got a couple hours' sleep in one of the cells in the back."

Whenever he saw her, Jesse felt like jumping up and wagging his tail. He always wanted to tell Jenn how beautiful she was and how much he loved her and how nothing she could do or say would shake him on that. And the strain of not doing that, which both he and Dix had agreed was in his best interest, was very burdensome.

"So what can you tell me about this murder," she said.

"On the record?"

Jenn paused for a minute, then she sighed a little.

"I hate when you ask me that," she said.

"I hate that I have to ask it," Jesse said.

Jenn nodded.

"But you do," she said. "I'm in my professional reporter costume, so, yes, we're on the record."

Jesse nodded.

"The body was discovered by Officer Luther Simpson...." Jesse said.

"That's Suit's real name?" Jenn said.

"Yep," Jesse said, "on routine patrol at approximately two a.m. this morning, on the front lawn of the Crowne estate on Paradise Neck. The victim has been identified as Fiona Francisco, who was a resident of Eleven Sewall Street in Paradise. While she lived there she was using the name Frances Franklin."

"Why the alias?" Jenn said.

"We don't know yet."

"How long she live there?"

"We're checking that. I'm guessing two, three years."

"Cause of death?"

"ME says two twenty-two-caliber bullets in the back of the head at close range."

"Was she killed at the Crowne estate?"

"At or close," Jesse said. "She bled a lot on the grass where they put her."

"Do you see any connection to the Crown estate school project, which drew protesters when it began?" Jenn said.

"None so far," Jesse said.

"Next of kin?"

"She has a daughter, Amber Francisco," Jesse said, "who called herself Alice Franklin while she lived here."

"Where are they from?"

"Don't know yet," Jesse said.

"Any leads?"

"Not yet."

"Any suspects?" Jenn said.

"Not yet."

"Can we do a stand-up on camera?" Jenn said.

"Nope."

"Oh, poo, Jesse," Jenn said. "Why not?"

"I don't ever recall getting in trouble by not talking," Jesse said. "Especially on camera."

She smiled.

"What about my career," she said.

Jesse sucked in his cheeks a little and did a bad impression of Clark Gable.

"Frankly, my dear," Jesse said, "I don't give a damn."

"I know," Jenn said.

They were quiet. Jesse was always puzzled by the fact that despite all her talkative charm and bubble, Jenn never revealed much of what she was thinking....*No, Jesse thought, of what she was* feeling.

"You know," Jesse said. "That's not true. I went for the easy joke. But it's not true."

"You do give a damn about my career?" she said.

"Yes," Jesse said. "There's self-interest in it. But if we are ever going to make it together, you have to be fully you."

"What did you say?"

"We can't..." He couldn't think exactly how to say it. "You can't care enough about me until you can care enough about you."

She stared at him in silence for what seemed to him a long time.

Finally she said, "I...I don't...I am very happy that you know that."

Jesse nodded.

"Give Dix the credit."

Jenn smiled.

"I already did," she said. "Is there anything off the record that you can tell me."

"Aha," Jesse said. "Putting it to the test already."

Jenn smiled again, and inclined her head.

"Well," she said. "Is there?"

"A lot," Jesse said.

Jenn took out a notebook, as Jesse started to talk.

When he was through she said, "So what's the connection between Crow and the Francisco family, and the Crowne estate?'

"I don't know," Jesse said.

"But you think there is one?"

"Give me something to investigate," Jesse said.

"What if it's a false lead?" Jenn said.

"Maybe I'll come across the real one in the process," Jesse said.

"Better than doing nothing?"

"The daughter, Amber, has a boyfriend who's a Hispanic gangster in Marshport," Jesse said. "The Crowne estate is a place where small Hispanic children are bused in from Marshport, despite local opposition. Amber's mother's body is found on the front lawn of the Crowne estate."

"Could be coincidence," Jenn said.

"Could be," Jesse said.

"But if I were on the story," Jenn said, "and I didn't follow up on the possible connection, they'd fire me."

Jesse nodded.

"What I don't get," Jenn said, "is Crow."

"Nobody entirely gets Crow," Jesse said.

"But if he doesn't want to kill the woman and return the girl, why doesn't he just go away?" Jenn said. "It's not like he hasn't done worse."

"Says he likes women."

Jenn nodded.

"You believe him?"

"He let those hostages off the boat ten years ago," Jesse said.

"And kept the money," Jenn said.

"Which he didn't have to split with anybody," Jesse said.

"So maybe it's just something he tells you," Jenn said. "That he likes women."

"Or tells himself," Jesse said.

"Or maybe it's true," Jenn said.

Jesse nodded.

"Or maybe it's true," he said.

36.

Crow had a bottle of champagne under his arm when he knocked on Marcy Campbell's door at 5:45 in the evening. When she answered the door, he held out the champagne.

"I thought we might want to drink this," Crow said, "and sort of close the circle."

"The one that opened with me tied up on the couch in my office?" Marcy said. "Some years ago?"

"Yep."

"What if I decline?"

"You keep the champagne, I go my way," Crow said.

"Well," Marcy said. "I decline."

"Enjoy the champagne," Crow said, and turned and walked toward the street.

Marcy stood in the doorway watching him. He reached her front gate and opened it when she said, "No."

Crow turned.

"No?"

"Don't go," Marcy said.

Crow nodded and let the gate swing shut and walked back.

"I just got home," Marcy said. "I need to take a shower."

"Sure," Crow said.

While she was gone, Crow found the kitchen and improvised an ice bucket out of a mixing bowl. He popped the cork on the champagne, poured some into a wineglass, put the rest of the bottle on ice, and took it to the living room. He sat and sipped the champagne he'd poured and looked at the room. Colonial American antiques, braided rugs, pine paneling, pictures of sailboats. Very New England. He finished his champagne as Marcy appeared in the bedroom door wearing a white robe.

"Want some champagne first?" Crow said.

"No," Marcy said.

"Okay," Crow said.

He walked into the bedroom and took off his shirt. He was wearing a gun, which he took from the holster and placed on the bed-side table. Then he took off the rest of his clothes. Marcy watched, standing by the bed.

"What's the scar from?" she said.

Crow shook his head. Marcy nodded and shrugged out of the robe. They looked at each other for a moment, then Marcy went to him and kissed him and half fell backward onto the bed. Crow went with her, ending up on the side near the nightstand, where his gun was.

Later they sat in the early-American living room, Crow with his clothes back on, Marcy in her white robe, and drank the cham-pagne.

"How'd you know," Marcy said.

"We know things," Crow said.

"We?"

"Apache warriors," Crow said.

"Are you really an Apache?"

"Yes."

"And you knew I wanted this," she said.

"Yes," Crow said, and smiled. "And if I was wrong, what'd I lose?"

"A hundred-dollar bottle of champagne," Marcy said.

"Three hundred," Crow said.

Marcy smiled.

"So maybe all that Apache warrior stuff is crap," she said.

"Maybe," Crow said.

"But maybe not?" Marcy said.

"You'd like it to be real," Crow said. "Wouldn't you?"

"Yes," Marcy said. "I would."

"It's real to me," Crow said.

"I only ever wanted to do this once," Marcy said.

Crow nodded.

"I'd rather it not happen again," Marcy said.

"Okay," Crow said.

"Don't think it wasn't wonderful," Marcy said.

"I don't think that," Crow said.

"I had a fantasy and I fulfilled it."

"Sure," Crow said.

"You understand?" Marcy said.

"Sure."

The champagne was gone. Crow looked at the empty bottle and stood.

"Time to go," he said.

Marcy nodded. They walked to the door together. At the door Marcy put her arms around him and then kissed him hard.

"Good-bye," she said.

"Good-bye," Crow said, and walked out and closed the door.

37.

Miriam Fiedler invited Jesse for lunch at the Paradise Yacht Club. In honor of the occasion Jesse wore a blue blazer.

"Well," Miriam said when he joined her at a table on the veranda with a view across the harbor to the town. "You dressed up, I'm flattered."

"The blazer covers up my gun," Jesse said.

Miriam continued to smile brightly.

"I love this view of the town," she said, "don't you?"

"Yes," Jesse said.

A young waitress came to the table. Miriam ordered a Manhattan. Jesse had iced tea.

"You don't drink, Chief Stone?" Miriam said.

"I do," Jesse said. "But generally not at lunch."

"Oh, no one would even notice," Miriam said. "All of the members have a drink at lunch."

Jesse nodded.

"Well, I see that I have my work cut out for me," Miriam said.

"How so?" Jesse said.

"You're not much of a talker."

"As soon as I know the topic," Jesse said, "I'll jump right in."

"Why are you so sure there's a topic?"

"Last week you were rooting for my death," Jesse said. "Now lunch. There's a topic."

"Oh, Chief Stone," Miriam said. "Of course there is. I don't know why I pretended there wasn't. May I call you Jesse. Everyone seems to."

"You may," Jesse said.

"Please call me Miriam."

"Okay," Jesse said.

"Because I'm passionate about the issue," Miriam said. "I realize I've been far too stri-

dent in the matter of the Crowne estate, and
I wish first to apologize."

"Good," Jesse said.

Miriam drank some of her Manhattan. Not
like someone who needed it, Jesse noticed,
merely like someone who liked it.

"And I wondered if we could find a way to
join forces, as it were, to confront a problem
which is now a mutual one."

She wasn't that bad-looking, Jesse thought.
Probably fiftysomething. Skin good. Slim, well-
dressed, well-groomed, and her teeth were
very white. She wore quite a bit of makeup
and was quite artful with it. Jesse remembered how clever Jenn had been with makeup.
He always paid attention to it in women.

"What would that problem be?" Jesse
said.

"The murder," Miriam said, her voice full of
surprise. "Murder on the very front lawn of
that lovely estate."

Jesse waited.

"Well, surely you see the connection," Miriam said. "Once that element penetrates a
town, then inevitably the crime rate soars,
and the fundamental value of a beautiful res-
idential town simply disappears."

"Obviously," Jesse said, "you're not claiming

that one of those preschool kids shot Fiona Francisco."

"No, no, of course not. But once it starts, like the tiny trickle that overwhelms the dike ... it's a tragedy," she said.

"Why do you think Fiona Francisco was killed by a Latino person?" Jesse said.

"Well, she was there on the front lawn, and obviously she wasn't killed by someone in Paradise."

"But you have no actual evidence," Jesse said.

"It's as plain as the nose on your face," she said.

Jesse nodded thoughtfully.

"That plain," he said. "What do you think I should do?"

"Well, first of all, close down that school. It will send them a message," Miriam said.

"I really have no right to close down a school," Jesse said.

"You have an obligation to protect us," Miriam said.

"I do," Jesse said.

He picked up the menu.

"What's good here," Jesse said.

Miriam stared at him.

"I'm not through talking," she said.

"I'm not surprised," Jesse said.

"Well, what are you going to do about this?"

Jesse put down the menu.

"I'll tell you what I'm not going to do," Jesse said. "I'm not going to sit here and talk ragtime with you. You have your reasons for wanting that school closed. But we both know they have little to do with the murder of Fiona Francisco."

"That's insulting," Miriam said.

"Yeah, I thought it might be," Jesse said. "Thanks for the iced tea."

He stood and walked through the open French doors, through the dining room, and out of the Yacht Club.

38.

Jesse stood with Jenn and Nina Pinero at the foot of the long, sloping lawn of the Crowne estate. At the top of the slope the children sat on the floor of the big front porch while one of the two teachers read them a book.

"Kids know about the murder?" Jesse said.

"Vaguely," Nina said.

"Press?" Jesse said.

"We've been able to keep them away pretty well." She looked at Jenn. "Until now."

"I'm Jenn Stone," Jenn said, "Channel Three News."

"Stone?" Nina said. "Any relation?"

"We used to be married," Jesse said.

"Does that give her special status?" Nina said.

"Yes," Jesse said. "It does."

"I won't bother the children," Jenn said. "I'm just gathering background for a larger story I'm working on."

"Didn't you used to do weather?" Nina said.

Jenn grinned at her.

"Sure did. Want some information on cold fronts and high-pressure systems?"

Nina smiled.

"No," she said. "I very much don't."

"No one seems to," Jenn said. "Except program directors and station managers."

"I would prefer you not talk to the children," Nina said.

"No need," Jenn said. "I have a lot of film from the first day they arrived."

"Nina," Jesse said. "Do I recall you saying that one of these Crowne estate kids had a brother in the Horn Street Boys?"

Nina looked at Jenn.

"This conversation is off the record," Nina said.

"Of course," Jenn said.

"Yes," Nina said to Jesse, "there's a brother."

"What's his name?"

"Why do you want to know?"

"The Horn Street Boys have a connection to the victim," Jesse said, "and a connection to the school. And the victim was found on school grounds."

"You think the Horn Street Boys are involved?"

"I only know what I told you," Jesse said. "I don't even have a theory yet."

"I won't give you a name," Nina said. "I shouldn't have even mentioned the brother."

"Why?" Jenn said.

"Improving life for these kids is so fragile a proposition," she said. "Anything can ruin us."

"Like having the head person in this program rat one of their brothers to the cops," Jesse said.

"Just like that," Nina said.

"But since you know of the relationship, the two boys must have some regular contact," Jesse said.

"Yes."

"So it's possible," Jesse said, "that the Horn Street Boys know abut the Crowne estate

project and maybe even about the local opposition."

"Yes."

"You think they were making a statement?"
Jenn said.

"I have no idea," Nina said.

"We're not the enemy," Jenn said. "We're
just trying to help."

"That may be true," Nina said. "But what I
said is also true. I don't know anything more
about the Horn Street Boys than what I've
told you."

Jesse said, "Thank you, Nina," and turned
and walked toward his car. Jenn lingered a
moment, and then said, "Thank you," and followed Jesse.

"That wasn't very productive," Jenn said,
as they drove back across the causeway.

"I had to confirm what was a very passing
remark, make sure I heard it right, so I'm not
wasting time with a theory that isn't so."

"Meticulous," Jenn said.

"It's mostly what the work is about," Jesse
said. "Keeping track of stuff."

"I wonder why people like Nina are so hos-
tile to the media," Jenn said.

"You and Nina have different goals," Jesse

said. "Even in the best case, you are trying to get at the truth. She is trying to salvage a few kids."

"Are the two incompatible?" Jenn said.

"Sometimes, yes," Jesse said. "Sometimes, no. People like Nina are intensely aware of the incompatible possibility."

"You said 'best case.' What's a worse case?"

"That your goal is not truth but advertising revenue," Jesse said.

Jenn smiled.

"Oh," she said. "That."

39.

They were sitting on a bench by the marina five blocks from Horn Street, looking at the boats, sharing a can of Pepsi and a joint.

"You know how to get to Florida?" Esteban said.

"Florida?" Amber said.

"I'm supposed to take you to Florida," Esteban said. "And I don't know where it is."

"What do you mean?" Amber said.

"Your old man's giving me ten thousand dollars to bring you down."

"I don't want to go to Florida."

"It's ten thousand dollars, baby," Esteban said.

"You gonna sell me to my father?" she said.

"No, no. I just bring you down, turn you over, he gives me the ten grand. I wait around a couple days. You run away and we come back up here. How long's it take to get to Florida?"

"I won't go," she said.

"Yeah, baby, you will," Esteban said. "Up front beside me, or in the trunk, either way you gonna go. Ten thousand dollars's a lot of money."

She looked at him in silence for a moment. Then she began to cry.

"Hey," Esteban said. "Hey, hey. This is for us, baby. You spend a couple fucking days with the old man, and we're outta there with the money."

Amber stood and ran. Esteban went after her, out along Marshport Way along the water. A hundred yards up from the marina was a red light. A half-painted, half-primed pickup truck that might once have been blue was stopped at the light. The back was full of loose copper pipe. Amber reached it as the light turned green and as the car started to move Amber stepped up onto the running board and hooked her arm through the window.

A big guy in a black tank top and a do-rag sat in the passenger seat. He had a thick gold chain around his neck.

"What the fuck are you doing," he said.

"Somebody's after me," she said. "Keep going."

The driver was a wiry kid with longish blond hair, tattoos on both forearms, and the scruffy beginnings of a beard.

"Keep going, hell," he said. "Whyn't we stop and clean his clock?"

"No, please, keep going," Amber said.

The driver looked in the rearview mirror.

"Hell," he said. "He's given up anyway. Lemme stop and you can get in."

She rode in the front seat between them, still crying.

"What's going on?" the big guy asked.

"I can't tell you," Amber said.

The big guy shrugged.

"Where you want to go?" the big guy said. "Want us to take you to the cops?"

"No," she said. "I...I want to go to Paradise."

"You want to take her to Paradise?" the big guy said to the driver.

"Sure," the driver said. "Better than running copper pipe all day."

40.

Crow came into the Paradise police station with Amber.

"Where the hell did you get her?" Molly said.

"She called me," Crow said. "From the shopping center."

"Paradise Mall?" Molly said.

Crow nodded.

"How'd she have your number?" Molly said.

"I gave it to her," Crow said. "When you cut her loose."

Molly looked at him for a moment and shook her head, and then looked at Amber.

Amber's eye makeup was ruined again by crying. She wore lace-up black boots, and black jeans that had been cut off very short, and a tank top with some kind of heavy-metal logo that Molly didn't recognize.

"How ya doing, Amber?"

Amber shook her head, looking down at the floor.

"He was going to make me go back to my father," she said.

"Who was?"

"My boyfriend," Amber said.

"And your boyfriend is?" Molly said.

Amber shook her head.

"Where is your father?" Molly said.

"Florida."

"Why was your boyfriend going to make you go back?" Molly said.

"My father paid him," Amber said.

"And what are you doing here?" Molly said.

"I ran away."

"And you called Crow," Molly said.

"He said he wouldn't make me go back," Amber said.

Molly looked at Crow again. Crow shrugged.

"So," Molly said to both of them, "what do you need from me?"

Amber continued to look at the floor. She shook her head and didn't speak.

"Stone around?" Crow said.

"He's not here at the moment," Molly said. "You're welcome to wait."

"Can I talk with you while I'm waiting?" Crow said.

"Sure."

"What about her?" Crow said.

"We can put her in a cell," Molly said.

"I don't want to be in jail," Amber said softly to the floor.

"Just a guest," Molly said. "Cell won't be locked. You can lie down, take a nap, if you wish."

Amber didn't say anything.

"You'll be safe there," Molly said. "Until we figure out a better arrangement."

Amber nodded faintly.

"We're going to keep you safe," Molly said. "I promise you."

"Take the cell," Crow said to Amber.

Amber said, "Okay."

Molly walked her back to the little cell block in the back of the station. There were four cells, all empty. The last one had a curtain made from a blanket that could be pulled across the door.

"This is where we usually put women," Molly said. "Give you a little privacy."

Amber went in and sat on the cot. There was a sink and a toilet.

"I'll leave the door open," Molly said, "and close the curtain. You need anything, come see me."

Amber nodded. Molly went back to the front desk.

"She jumps pretty quick when you speak," Molly said.

"She knows I mean it," Crow said.

Molly nodded. Crow was wearing a faded tan safari shirt with short sleeves. Molly was fascinated with the play of intricate muscles in his arms.

"So what do you think we're going to do with her?" Molly said.

"Her mother's dead," Crow said. "She doesn't want to go back to her father. She's on the run from her boyfriend."

"So you don't want to look out for her?"

"That's what I'm doing now," Crow said.

"We can't keep her here until she's like twenty-one," Molly said. "I mean, she can't live in the jail."

"Maybe we can figure something out," he said.

Molly nodded. They were quiet. Crow seemed comfortable with quiet. *He's all angles and planes,* Molly thought, *like some kind of really good machine, where everything works perfectly.* His eyes were black and seemed to penetrate everything. Molly felt as if he could see through her clothes. It was almost embarrassing.

"Why do you care?" Molly said to Crow.

"I feel like it," Crow said.

"You care because you feel like caring?"

"Yes."

"What if you didn't feel like it?"

"Then I wouldn't," Crow said.

He smiled at her.

"I know who you are," Molly said. "And I know what you do. Actually, you probably do worse than what I know."

"Much," Crow said.

"But there seems to be this streak of— What? Chivalry?—running through it."

"Maybe," Crow said.

"You like women."

"Yes."

"Why?"

Crow's eyes held on her. She felt herself blushing. Crow smiled.

"Besides that," Molly said.

"That's plenty," Crow said.

"But is that all?" Molly said.

"Trying to figure me out is a waste of time," he said.

"Have you figured you out?" Molly said.

"I know what I feel like doing," Crow said. "And what I don't."

"Is that enough?" Molly said.

"Yes," Crow said. "It is."

Again, Molly had the odd feeling that she was naked under his gaze. It was a puzzling feeling. *It's even more puzzling,* she thought, *that maybe I like it.*

41.

"Amber Francisco is here," Molly said when Jesse came into the station.

"Why?"

"Crow brought her in," Molly said.

"Where is he?"

"He left," Molly said. "Told me he'd check in with you later."

"Where is she?" Jesse said.

"In back," Molly said. "In the women's cell."

"Let's go see her," Jesse said.

"You want me to fill you in first?" Molly said.

"Nope. I'd rather start fresh. We'll talk with

her and you can compare what she says to what you know."

Molly nodded and walked with Jesse back to the curtained cell. Molly pulled the curtain aside and looked in.

Amber was lying on her side with her legs bent and her eyes closed. She had washed her face and looked much younger.

"Amber?" Molly said. "You awake?"

Amber opened her eyes and didn't speak. Molly nodded and pulled the curtain aside and she and Jesse went in. Amber stared at them without moving.

"You remember me, Amber?" Jesse said.

She didn't say anything.

"If we're going to work this out, you'll need to talk. You may as well start now," Jesse said. "You remember me?"

"Yes."

"You know who I am?"

"Yes."

"How did you get here?"

"Guys in a pickup truck brought me from Marshport."

She remained lying on her side. Her face held no animation. Her voice was flat.

"How come?" Jesse said.

"My boyfriend was gonna sell me back to my father."

"Your boyfriend is Esteban Carty?"

She didn't answer.

"What's your boyfriend's name?" Jesse said.

She shook her head.

"Did he kill your mother?"

She didn't answer.

"Why won't you talk about him?" Jesse said.

"I won't," Amber said.

"Why not?"

"I don't know."

"Do you know who killed your mother?"

She didn't answer.

"Do you?" Jesse said.

"No."

"Why did you call Crow?" Jesse said.

She shrugged, which, Jesse thought, might not be easy lying on your side.

"You think he'd protect you from your boyfriend?"

"I had his phone number," she said.

"And you thought he'd protect you?"

"I thought Esteban would be afraid of him."

"Your boyfriend," Jesse said. "Esteban?"

"No. I didn't mean Esteban. My boyfriend is another man."

"But you said 'Esteban.'"

"No," she said.

Jesse nodded.

"You could have called us," he said.

"The police?"

"Uh-huh, nine-one-one would have done it."

"I was afraid you'd arrest me."

"Arrest you for what?" Jesse said.

"I don't know," she said. "For nothing...that's what cops do."

"Why don't you want to go back to your father?" Jesse said.

"He's creepy," Amber said. "He's got all these creepy guys around. And he'll make me go to school with the nuns. Nuns are creepy."

Jesse nodded.

"What's your father do for a living?" Jesse said.

"He does a lot of stuff. He makes a lot of money. But he's creepy."

"Any of the creepy guys around him bother you any?" Jesse said.

"Yeah."

"You ever tell him?"

"He told me to shut up and not talk dirty."

Jesse nodded.

"So you have a plan?"

"Plan?"

"Yeah," Jesse said. "Where you're going to live. What you're going to do for work."

She looked at him silently with her eyes wide and empty for a long time.

Then she said, "I don't have no plan."

"Well, you can bunk here for the moment until we work out something better," Jesse said. "You want something to eat?"

"I don't know."

Jesse nodded as if that made sense.

"Moll," he said. "Get whoever's on patrol to stop by Daisy's and pick up a couple sandwiches."

"Can I have ice cream?" Amber said.

"What kind?"

"Chocolate?"

"Sure," Jesse said.

He looked at Molly.

"Coming up," Molly said.

42.

The Paradise police firing range was out-
doors, backing up to some wetlands and
shielded by dirt bunkers that had been bull-
dozed. Jesse had a new Smith & Wesson
.40-caliber semiautomatic handgun that he
wanted to break in. He had his earmuffs off,
reloading a magazine, when Crow parked on
the street and walked through the short trail
into the firing area.

"Officer Molly told me you were here,"
Crow said.

Jesse nodded.

"You want to shoot?" he said.

"Sure," Crow said. "Can I borrow a gun?"

Jesse smiled.

"You got a gun," Jesse said.

"It is illegal to carry a gun in this state without a permit," Crow said.

"You'd have a gun in the shower," Jesse said.

Crow smiled and spread his hands. Jesse nodded.

"In this town it is legal for someone to carry a gun to the firing range and shoot with the chief of police," Jesse said.

Crow looked steadily at Jesse for a moment. Then he nodded once, took a Glock nine-millimeter off his hip, crouched slightly, and, holding the Glock in both hands, put six rounds into the center of the target. Jesse finished loading the Smith & Wesson, turned sideways, and, firing with one hand, put six rounds into the center of the target.

"We're good," Crow said.

"We are."

"You fire like an old-time target shooter," Crow said.

"My father taught me that," Jesse said.

"Whatever works," Crow said.

Jesse put the Smith & Wesson down, and took his little .38 Chief's Special off his hip.

"You can hit the target with that thing?" Crow said.

"Sometimes," Jesse said. He began to crank the target toward them. "Especially if it's closer."

"Most shooting is close," Crow said.

"Yes," Jesse said, and put three rounds into the middle of the target.

"You didn't empty the weapon," Crow said.

"Neither did you," Jesse said.

"We're careful," Crow said.

"Got anything to tell me about Amber Francisco and friends?" Jesse said.

"Nothing I didn't tell Officer Molly," Crow said.

"And you got any thoughts on what we're gonna do with her?" Jesse said.

"You're the serve-and-protect guy," Crow said.

"You can't look out for her," Jesse said.

"'Course not," Crow said.

"You got any thoughts on who killed her mother?" Jesse said.

"Probably Esteban," Crow said.

"Why?"

"Figure if he's talking to her daddy about bringing her to Florida, he may have talked to her daddy about killing her mother."

Jesse nodded.

"So why doesn't she say so?"

"Scared?" Crow said.

"Probably," Jesse said. "Loyal."

"Loyal?" Crow said. "He sold her out."

"She's got nothing else," Jesse said. "She can tell herself she loves him, and maybe convince herself that he loves her, she won't feel so alone."

"And this is better than going back to Daddy?" Crow said.

"Apparently."

"He must be fun," Crow said.

"So what're your plans," Jesse said.

"I'm considering my options," Crow said.

"Would one of those be to get out of town?" Jesse said.

"Not yet," Crow said.

"Why not," Jesse said.

"Unfinished business," Crow said.

"You want to see this through with the kid?"

"Something like that," Crow said.

"Let's not get in each other's way," Jesse said.

"Sure," Crow said

Jesse put the .38 back on his hip and the .40 in a small gym bag with two boxes of ammunition.

"You gonna pick up the brass?" Crow said.

"No," Jesse said.

"Great to be chief," Crow said.

43.

Molly and Jesse were in the squad room, drinking coffee.

"I'm sorry, Jesse," Molly said. "I can't take her."

"I know," Jesse said.

"I have a husband and four kids. I can't impose her on them."

"I know," Jesse said. "I guess I'll have to take her."

"Yourself?"

"Can't have her living here," Jesse said.

"You can't bring a fourteen-year-old girl home to live with you, Jesse, alone."

Jesse shrugged.

"I mean, what if she claims you molested her?" Molly said.

"I'll claim I didn't," Jesse said.

"But even if you can prove you didn't, that kind of thing will cling to you for life," Molly said. "It's not like this is a good kid. You can't tell what she'll do."

"I know."

"So, what about that female private detective you were dating?"

"Sunny Randall?"

"Yes. How about you get her to look after the kid."

Jesse shook his head.

"That book is closed," Jesse said. "Right now, I don't want to open it again."

"You cannot take her in alone," Molly said. "What if she's sick, what if...you just can't be parenting a fourteen-year-old girl that's not your daughter."

"Got any ideas?" Jesse said.

"How about Human Services?"

"This is not just a runaway kid," Jesse said. "Dangerous people are after her. You can't ask some social worker to fight it out with the Horn Street Boys...or whoever her old man sends."

"You think he'll send someone?"

"Crow thinks so," Jesse said.

"And you think he's right?" Molly said.

"Louis Francisco doesn't seem to be the kind of guy who would let Crow double-cross him, or allow his daughter to leave when he wanted her home."

"Maybe you should talk to that detective you met from Fort Lauderdale," Molly said. "Kelly something."

"Cruz," Jesse said. "Kelly Cruz. I already talked to her. She, too, says Francisco is the man in South Florida. Says she's going to talk to a Miami cop named Ray Ortiz about him, see what she can learn."

"So helpful," Molly said. "Did you sleep with her?"

"No," Jesse said.

"Wow," Molly said. "A rare exception."

"Doesn't mean I won't," Jesse said.

Molly grinned.

"I like your spirit," she said.

Jesse stood and got the coffeepot and poured some in Molly's cup and some in his own. Molly stirred some Splenda into hers.

"Jenn," Molly said.

Jesse put the coffeepot back and came

and sat down. He poured some sugar from a yellow cardboard box and stirred it into his coffee.

"Jenn," he said.

"It would be her chance," Molly said, "to be personally involved in a real human-interest story, or a murder, or a gang war, or an arrest, or however it turns out.... *Here's Jenn Stone, Channel Three News, with the inside story.*"

"She might be in danger," Jesse said.

"Explain that to her, let her decide."

"I don't want her in danger," Jesse said.

"Jesse," Molly said, and paused, and then went on, "that would be for her to decide, I think."

Jesse didn't say anything. Molly and he each drank some coffee. The sun was hitting them both in the eyes through the east window of the room. Jesse got up and pulled the shade and came back and sat down and looked at Molly.

"I think you're probably right," he said.

44.

Four men wearing flowered shirts flew up from Miami on Delta. They picked up a Cadillac Escalade from a rental agency, drove to a motel on Marshport Road, and registered, two in a room. A half-hour after they arrived, an Asian man came to the door of one of the rooms with a big shopping bag that said Cathay Gardens on it.

One of the men from Miami opened the door. He was tall and straight and had salt-and-pepper hair.

"Mr. Romero?" said the man with the Cathay Gardens bag.

"Yes."

The delivery man held out the bag. Romero took it, gave him a hundred-dollar bill, and closed the door. Romero's roommate was a squat bald man named Larson.

"What did we get?" Larson said.

Romero took the bag to the bed and opened it. He took out some cartons of Chinese food, four semiautomatic pistols, and four boxes of ammunition. Romero checked. All the guns were loaded. Larson opened one of the cartons.

"May as well eat the food," he said.

At 4:40 in the afternoon, the four men from Miami parked the Escalade at the head of Horn Street and got out. Parked a half-block away, on the corner of Nelson Boulevard, Crow watched them go down the alley. He smiled.

Didn't take long, he thought.

At 12A Horn Street, Romero knocked on the door. Esteban answered.

"You Carty?" Romero said.

"Yes."

"So where's the girl?" Romero said.

"You from Mr. Francisco?" Esteban said.

Romero nodded.

"He wants to know about the girl," Romero said.

Esteban jerked his head and stepped aside and the four men went in. There were half a dozen Horn Street Boys inside. The four men from Miami ignored them.

"I was just about to bring her over there," Esteban said.

"Over where?"

"To Florida," Esteban said. "And she run off."

"Where'd she go?"

"I don't know. Paradise, maybe," Esteban said. "That's where she lived with her old lady."

"Next town," Romero said.

"Yeah," Esteban said. "I didn't think she'd run off."

"But she did," Romero said.

"I did a good job on the old lady, didn't I?" Esteban said.

"And you got paid," Romero said. "Now we want the girl."

"I can take you over there," Esteban said. "Show you where she lived with her old lady."

Romero nodded.

"How about a guy named Cromartie, calls himself Crow?" Romero said.

"That sonovabitch," Esteban said.

"He in Paradise, too, you think?"

"Yeah, man," Esteban said. "He's there. Maybe got the girl, too. Okay with me you take the girl. But not Crow. I want him for myself."

Romero smiled.

"You think you can handle him?" Romero said.

"He killed one of us," Esteban said. "You kill a Horn Street Boy, you got to kill them all."

Romero shrugged.

"I don't care who kills him as long as somebody does. Mr. Francisco wants him dead."

"He pay somebody to do it?" Esteban said.

"You think we're up here for the hell of it?" Romero said.

"Maybe I get there first, I get the ten thousand."

"Ten thousand," Romero said.

"That's what I got for the old lady," Esteban said.

Romero nodded.

"That's what I was going to get for the girl," Esteban said. "Maybe still will, I get there first."

"Twenty grand," Romero said. "Set for life."

"You gotta problem with that?" Esteban said.

"I got a problem," Romero said, "you'll be the first to know."

"I got a right to that money," Esteban said.

Romero looked at him for a moment, then he shook his head and turned and went out. The other three men from Miami followed him.

45.

Jesse sat in his living room with Amber and Jenn. Jesse had scotch. Jenn had a glass of wine. Amber was drinking coffee. She was wearing the same clothes she'd come to the jail in, and the same tear-streaked eye makeup.

"I can drink booze," Amber said.

"Not with me," Jesse said.

Amber was looking around the condo.

"How long I gotta stay here?" she said.

"You don't have to stay here at all," Jesse said. "You can leave right now...but where you gonna go?"

"I could find someone to stay with," Amber said.

"You have someone to stay with," Jesse said.

"You?"

"Me."

"Why's she here," Amber said.

"Jenn and I used to be married," Jesse said. "She's come to help me with you."

"Why do you need help with me?" Amber said.

"Because you're a fourteen-year-old girl and there needs to be a woman here, too," Jesse said.

"Oh, man, are you drab."

"Drab," Jesse said.

"Who cares about who stays with who. Man, try being free, you know? Jesus."

"Jenn is a television reporter," Jesse said. "She's doing this in hopes of a story."

"Story about what," Amber said.

"About you," Jenn said. "And your parents. And the Horn Street Boys. And maybe the Crown estates project . . . like that."

"What the hell kind of story is that?" Amber said.

"We'll see," Jenn said. "I had some vacation

time coming and the station gave me a couple weeks to see if there was a story."

"So am I gonna be on TV?" Amber said.

"We'll see," Jenn said.

"I don't want to go to my father," Amber said.

"Okay," Jesse said.

"And I don't want to go back to Esteban, the lying fuck."

"Okay there, too," Jesse said. "I've been talking to a friend who's a lawyer, and she's going to put me in touch with specialists in child custody and placement."

"Child custody? I'm not in fucking child custody," Amber said.

"Officer Molly Crane will be with you and Jenn much of the day," Jesse said to Amber. "I will be with you most of the rest of the time. Occasionally, one of the other cops may fill in. There will always be a police officer with you."

"So my old man won't get me," she said. "Or Esteban."

"Or anyone else," Jesse said.

"What about Crow?" Amber said.

"What about him?"

"Is he gonna be around?"

"Crow pretty much does what he wants to," Jesse said. "If I see him, I'll ask him."

"So what am I supposed to do all day while you're all watching me?"

"What would you like to do?" Jesse said.

"I don't know."

"There's a start," Jesse said. "How about taking a shower?"

"Here?"

"Yes."

"I got no clean clothes," Amber said.

"Tomorrow you and Jenn and Molly can go buy some. Meanwhile, you can wear one of my shirts for a nightie."

"What should I do with my other clothes?"

"We could burn them in the fireplace," Jesse said.

"Throw them out of the bathroom," Jenn said. "I'll put them through the washer."

"Another thing we have to consider," Jesse said. "Jenn will be in my bedroom. Amber will be in the guest room. I will be on the couch. There is one bathroom."

"So?" Amber said.

"So keep it in mind," Jesse said.

"How come you and her don't sleep together?" Amber said.

"Too drab," Jesse said.

46.

Suitcase Simpson came into Jesse's office and closed the door and sat down in a chair facing Jesse. His face was red, and he seemed to be looking steadily at the top of Jesse's desk.

Jesse waited.

Suit didn't say anything.

Jesse waited.

"I'm having sex with an older woman," Suit said.

"Miriam Fiedler," Jesse said.

Suit raised his eyes.

"How'd you know that?" he said.

Jesse shrugged.

"I'm the chief of police," Jesse said.

"Molly told you," Suit said.

"No," Jesse said. "She didn't."

Suit looked back at the desktop.

"Suit," Jesse said. "Mostly, I don't care what you do with your dick when you're off duty."

"I know," Suit said.

"So?"

"So she's asking me a bunch of questions," Suit said.

"About?"

"You, the department, the Crown estate deal," Suit said.

"Like what?"

"Were you a good cop," Suit said. "Did I think you'd ever take a bribe? Did you have a relationship with Nina Pinero? Was it true you were fired in L.A.? What's going on with you and Jenn? She wanted to know anything I knew about the murder. Did I think there was any Hispanic involvement?"

"Concerned citizen," Jesse said.

"I figured you should know."

Jesse nodded.

"She is very committed to this problem," he said.

"She is," Suit said.

"Why?" Jesse said.

"Real-estate values?"

Jesse shrugged.

"Maybe," he said. "Seems awful important to her."

"You think there might be something more?"

"Maybe," Jesse said. "How's she compare to Mrs. Hathaway?"

Suit reddened again.

"Come on, Jesse."

"No kiss-and-tell?" Jesse said.

"Or whatever," Suit said.

"Good boy," Jesse said.

"Miriam says so, too," Suit said. "Want me to break it off?"

Jesse shook his head.

"I'd like you to stay with it," Jesse said.

Suit grinned.

"Undercover, so to speak," he said.

"So to speak," Jesse said. "See what else you can learn."

Suit grinned again.

"Tough dirty work..." Suit said.

Jesse nodded.

"But somebody's got to do it," he said.

47.

Romero was driving. Esteban was beside him. Two men from Miami were in the backseat, and Larson was way back in the third seat.

"Cromartie lives someplace called Strawberry Cove," Romero said.

"In Paradise?" Esteban said.

"Yeah. You know where that is?"

Esteban shook his head. Romero shrugged and reached his hand back over the seat. One of the men from Miami opened a briefcase and took out a sheet of paper. Romero looked at it.

"Off Breaker Avenue," he said to Esteban. "You know where that is?"

"No," Esteban said. "How you guys know this?"

"We checked," Romero said. "You think we just jumped on a plane and come up here to mill around?"

"But how did you check?" Esteban said. "Ain't it a long way?"

"The town paper prints a summary of the week's real-estate transactions every Thursday."

"You can get the Paradise paper over there?" Esteban said.

"We got people to do it for us," Romero said.

He punched the navigation system that came with the car, and in a moment the directions came up. Esteban stared at it.

"How far you been from Horn Street, kid?" Romero asked.

"I ain't no kid," Esteban said. "I'm twenty years old, man."

"How far you been?"

"Got no reason to go far," Esteban said. "Got all I need right there. Got my boys. Got pussy, beer, wheeze. Nobody fucks with us. Got no reason to leave."

"Ever kill anybody, Esteban?" Romero said.

"Hey, man, I just scragged the old lady a little while ago, you know that."

"Ever kill anybody who could kill you?" Romero said.

"Shit, man, what are you saying? I kill anybody needs to be killed, man. I ain't scared."

"You recognize Cromartie if you see him?"

"I'll recognize the cocksucker."

"Good," Romero said. "You see him, you tell me."

"You gonna kill him?"

"Yes," Romero said. "We are."

"You don't know what he looks like?" Esteban said.

"I do," Romero said.

"I can show you where little hot pants lives, too," Esteban said.

"Name's Amber," Romero said. "I don't think Mr. Francisco would like it to have you call her 'hot pants.'"

"Fuck him," Esteban said. "I say what I want."

Romero nodded.

"I don't much like it, either," Romero said.

"So fuck you, too," Esteban said. "You think I'm scared of you?"

From the backseat one of the men from Miami caught Romero's eye in the rearview mirror and made a shooting gesture with his forefinger and thumb at Esteban. Romero shook his head.

"Well," Romero said to Esteban, "you probably know what you're talking about."

"You got that right, man," Esteban said. "*Hot...Pants!* You want to see where she lives?"

"Be easier to take her to Miami," Romero said, "if we kill Crow first."

"Sure," Romero said, and turned left onto Breaker Avenue.

The men in the Escalade had no expectation of being followed, so it was easy enough for Crow to keep them in sight. When they took the turn onto Breaker Avenue, Crow smiled. He knew where they were going. When the Escalade parked in front of his condo, Crow drove on past them and turned left, away from the water, onto a side street a hundred yards up the road, and parked.

It was a condo neighborhood. No kids. Everyone working. The stillness was palpable. Crow got out of the car, walked to the corner of the street, leaned on a tall blue mail-deposit box, and looked back down toward his condo. The five men from the Escalade had gotten out and were standing on the small lawn in front of the four-unit building. Crow's unit was first floor left. The men spread out as they walked toward the door. Each had a handgun out, holding it inconspicuously down. *Pros,* Crow thought. *Not scared of much. Don't care if somebody sees them. Nobody home in the neighborhood anyway.*

The squat man with the bald head rang Crow's doorbell. The men waited. The bald man rang again. Then he looked at the tall man with the graying hair. The tall man said something and the bald man stepped back and kicked the door. It gave but not enough. He kicked it again and they were in.

Crow went back to his car, opened the trunk, selected a bolt-action Ruger rifle, and left the trunk ajar. He didn't check the load. He knew it was loaded. His weapons were always loaded. Crow saw no point to empty guns. Carrying the Ruger, Crow went back to the mailbox and rested the rifle on top of it. There were a couple of late-summer butterflies drifting about. And a dragonfly. Nothing else moved. In perhaps three minutes, the men filed out of Crow's broken front door. Their handguns were no longer visible. They headed for the Escalade.

Carefully, Crow rested his front elbow on

the mailbox and sighted the Ruger in on the bald man. *One's as good as another,* Crow thought. *Except Romero. Romero was the stud.* If he killed Romero the rest of them would go home. He took a breath, let it out, took up the trigger slack, and shot the bald man in the center of his chest. Then he went to his car, put the rifle into the trunk, latched the trunk, got in the front seat, and drove away. *Besides,* Crow said to himself, *he had the ugliest shirt.*

In front of the condo the men were crouched behind the Escalade. They had their guns out.

"Anyone see where it came from?" Romero said.

No one had. After a moment, Romero stood and walked to where Larson lay. He squatted and put his hand on Larson's neck. Then he stood and walked back to the Escalade.

"Let's go," he said.

They got in and drove away, leaving Larson quiet on the front lawn.

48.

They were all in the squad room, except Molly, who was with Amber, and Arthur, who was on the desk. There was coffee, and an open box of donuts. Jesse sat at the far end of the conference table.

"We're all on call now, all the time, until this thing shakes out," Jesse said. "I'll try to get you enough sleep. But if I can't, I can't."

No one spoke.

"Here's what we know," Jesse said. "The vic is a guy named Rico Larson. His driver's license says he lives in Miami. He was carrying a Glock nine when he was killed by one bullet from a .350 rifle. The shot probably came from about a hundred yards down the road and across the street. He was shot in front of a condominium town house rented by Wilson Cromartie."

Suitcase Simpson reached across the table for a donut.

"Crow," he said.

Jesse nodded.

"Everybody in that neighborhood works during the day," Jesse said. "No one saw anything. No one heard a shot."

"We got a theory of the crime?" Peter Perkins asked.

"Guy in Miami," Jesse said, "his wife ran away, took his daughter with her. Guy in Miami—name's Francisco—hired Crow to find them. So Crow found them... here. Daughter's got a boyfriend in Marshport, gang kid named Esteban Carty. Crow calls up Francisco, says, 'I found them, what do I do now?' Francisco says, 'Kill the mother, bring back the daughter.' Crow says, 'No.' This much I get from Crow, and it's probably true."

"You been talking to Crow?" Buddy Hall said.

"Yes."

"How come he didn't do what the Miami guy wanted?"

"Crow says he likes women," Jesse said. "And besides, he didn't feel like it."

"You believe that?" Cox said.

"I believe he didn't do it," Jesse said.

"So how about the mother," Cox said. "Did he kill her?"

"Crow? I don't think so. He says it was probably the gang kid, Esteban."

"That make any sense?" Peter Perkins said.

"Esteban made a deal to turn her over to her father," Jesse said. "Maybe he made a deal to kill the mother, too."

"Girl say that?"

"Nope."

"Wouldn't she rat out the guy that killed her mother?" Cox said.

"She didn't like her mother," Jesse said.

These were small-town guys, most of them not very old, Jesse knew, most of them very conventional. The idea that you wouldn't like your mother was hard for them. No one said anything.

"She doesn't like her father, either," Jesse said. "That's why she ran away when she found out Esteban was going to take her down there."

"She come here?" Peter Perkins said.

"Crow brought her in," Jesse said.

"Crow?" Cox said. "What is it with Crow?"

Jesse shook his head.

"What about this guy in Miami?" Paul Murphy said. "He a bad guy?"

"Big player in the South Florida rackets," Jesse said.

"So who's the dead guy?" Murphy said.

"Now, it's all theory," Jesse said. "I figure that Francisco sent him up to kill Crow, and bring the girl home."

"You think he came alone?"

"No one would send one guy after Crow," Jesse said. "Besides, there's no car. How did he get there?"

"You think Crow shot him?"

"Probably," Jesse said.

"And the other guys split," Murphy said.

"Yep."

"If Crow's as good as everybody thinks he is," Murphy said, "how come he didn't get more than one?"

Jesse was quiet for a moment, thinking about Crow.

Then he said, "Maybe he didn't want to."

"That's crazy," Peter Perkins said.

"Crow's not like other people," Jesse said. "Suit, you go down to my house and stay with Molly and the kid. I'll relieve you later. Everyone else, shotguns in every car, cleaned, loaded, no plastic daisies in the barrel. Extra ammo in every car, shotgun and handgun. Vests with you at all times."

"Jesus, Jesse," Suit said. "It sounds like you're expecting a war."

"Always possible," Jesse said.

49.

Jesse sat with Jenn on the balcony outside his living room and looked at the harbor as it got dark. Amber was standing in the doorway drinking coffee. She had on tan shorts and a powderblue T-shirt and too much makeup, but she was, Jesse thought, beginning to look a little less like a punk cliché.

"Have you done any research on the Crowne estate?" Jesse said.

He was sipping scotch. Jenn had a glass of Riesling.

"You mean the estate itself?" Jenn said.

"Yeah."

"No, you think I should?"

"Yes."

"Because?"

"Because you can and I don't have the resources," Jesse said.

"Why do you think it needs to be researched?" Jenn said.

"I think Miriam Fiedler's interest in the issue is too large," Jesse said.

"Explain," Jenn said.

"Suit says she's asking questions about me, and the department, and the murder, and can I be bribed."

"Suit?" Amber said. "The guy that was here with me and Molly?"

"Yes," Jesse said.

"Why would Miriam Fiedler be asking Suit questions?" Jenn said.

Jesse smiled. Jenn looked at him.

"Why?" Jenn said.

"Remember what I told you about Cissy Hathaway?" Jesse said. "Suit likes older women."

"Suit and Miriam Fiedler?" Jenn said.

"Suit's fucking somebody?" Amber said from the doorway.

"Well put," Jesse said.

"So maybe this Miriam Fiddler or whatever is fucking him so he'll tell her stuff," Amber said.

"Maybe," Jesse said.

"So," Amber said, "big deal. It happens all the time."

"You think?" Jesse said.

"How else do you get anything?" Amber said.

"Sometimes women have sex with men because they like them," Jenn said. "Even sometimes because they love them."

"Yeah, you bet," Amber said. "You like him?" She nodded at Jesse.

"Yes," Jenn said. "I probably love him."

"So how come you don't fuck him?"

"Right now it doesn't seem like a good idea," Jenn said.

"So you like him, but you won't fuck him. And you love him but you're divorced."

"That's about right," Jenn said.

"You ever fuck some guy to get what you want?" Amber said.

"Yes," Jenn said.

"See?" Amber said. "No big deal."

"It is a big deal," Jenn said. "Because every time you do it you feel weak and worthless."

"Maybe you do," Amber said. "Not me."

"You will," Jenn said. "It's cumulative."

"Huh?"

"The more of it you do," Jenn said, "the more you feel bad."

"I like it," Amber said. "When I'm balling a guy, I'm in charge, you know?"

"Like Esteban," Jesse said.

Amber didn't say anything for a moment. Then her eyes filled, and she turned and went through the living room to her bedroom.

"You hurt her feelings," Jenn said.

"Esteban hurt her feelings," Jesse said.

"And you reminded her of it."

"She can't be lying to herself," Jesse said. "How is that good for her?"

"Maybe she has so little else," Jenn said. "You ever see *The Ice Man Cometh*?"

"No."

Jenn shrugged.

"Doesn't matter," she said.

"My parenting skills are limited," Jesse said. "But I'm pretty sure the truth is good."

"Maybe it's not always," Jenn said.

"Maybe it isn't," Jesse said. "But I'm not too sure about lying, either."

"I know."

They were silent. Jesse sipped his scotch. Jenn stared out at the harbor, where the darkness had thickened enough so that the lights on some of the yachts were showing.

"I can check the legal stuff about the Crowne estate," Jenn said. "Deed, title, whatever. Hell, I can probably get an intern to do that."

"Might be useful," Jesse said.

"I'll see what I can find out," Jenn said. "Now I'm going in to the bedroom and pat Amber on the shoulder for a little bit."

"Maternal impulse?" Jesse said.

"Damned if I know," Jenn said, and went inside.

Jesse put his feet up on the railing and looked at the harbor. Across it the lights were going on in houses along Paradise Neck. Suppers were being cooked. Spouses were having a cocktail together while it cooked. Jesse looked at his moisture-beaded glass. He liked the look of it with the dark gold booze and the translucent silver ice. Still half-full. And he could have another if he wished. Two drinks was reasonable. And after the two drinks, he and Jenn and maybe Amber would have supper in a not distasteful caricature of the lives being lived across the harbor.

I wonder how much Crow drinks, Jesse thought.

50.

"It was Crow," Francisco said on the phone.

"I didn't see him," Romero said.

"It was Crow," Francisco said. "Forget about him. Get Amber and bring her home."

"He killed Larson," Romero said.

"There's a million other Larsons," Francisco said. "Bring the kid home."

"I don't like having some guy shoot one of my people and walk away," Romero said.

"I don't give a fuck what you like. Farm Crow out to the local gangbangers. Bring the kid home now."

"How much to the gangbangers?" Romero said.

"Ten, same as if they brought the kid home."

"Ten?" Romero said. "To kill Crow?"

"That's more money than they can even count," Francisco said. "How many are there?"

"Maybe a dozen," Romero said.

"So if Crow kills a few, no sweat," Francisco said. "Still plenty left to do the job."

"Ten grand," Romero said.

"And they'll be happy to get it," Francisco said. "Turn Crow over to them. Bring the kid home. We got a lot of business to do down here."

"Okay, Lou," Romero said.

The phone went dead. Romero folded his cell phone and slid it back in his pants pocket. He looked at the other two men, Bobby Chacon and a guy named Mongo Estella, for whom Bobby had to translate.

"We give the Crow hit to Esteban," Romero said to Bobby. "And bring the girl home."

"We know where the girl is?" Bobby said.

"No," Romero said.

Bobby nodded and spoke to Mongo in Spanish. Romero started the Escalade.

"First thing," Romero said, "we make the deal with Esteban and his people."

"You think they good enough?" Bobby said.

"No. But they are maybe crazy enough. Crazy might work better than good, with Crow."

Bobby nodded.

Driving carefully behind them, Crow was cautious. They would be looking for him now. But the Escalade was big and uncommon on the streets of Marshport, and Crow stayed with them easily enough. He was driving a grayish-beige Toyota, of which there were usually three or four in sight at all times. At Horn Street, the Escalade parked. Two of the men got out and walked down the alley. Crow turned right and then left and parked on a parallel street where he could see the Escalade through a parking lot. In ten minutes the two men came out onto Horn Street and got into the Escalade and drove east. Crow drove parallel for a couple of blocks and then swung up onto the same street several cars behind them. He followed them for a while and then turned off left, took the next right, followed them in a rough parallel course until he passed them and turned back to their street, coming out ahead of them. He drove ahead of them, watching them in the mirror until they turned off. Then he U-turned and fell in behind them on the road to Paradise.

The Escalade parked on Sewall Street, near the house where Fiona Francisco had lived. Crow parked up on Washington Street where he could see them. The same two men got out and went to the house. The front door was locked. There was a lot of foot traffic. After a moment the two men walked around the house and Crow couldn't see them. He waited. After about fifteen minutes the two men came back and got into the Escalade. The big car drove down Sewall Street and parked on the wharf outside the Gray Gull. All three men got out and went into the restaurant. Crow drove in and parked at the far end of the wharf.

Crow sat and looked at the restaurant, and in a short while the three men appeared on the outside deck and sat at a table. Crow sank a little lower in the front seat of his car so that he could just see through the steering wheel. They had a drink. They read the menus. Crow studied them. Why had they gone to the house? Were they looking for him? No. They wouldn't look for him there. They were looking for the girl. If they found her, they'd take her straight to Miami. So who was going to kill him? Francisco would not let it slide. It wasn't how he worked. No one was allowed to cross him.

Crow sat in his car and watched the men drink and eat on the deck. He could probably step out of the car and kill all three of them...too easy. Crow wanted the war to evolve a little. Such a good opportunity, though. He got out and walked between the parked cars to the near edge of the wharf. Across about ten feet of harbor water he fired one shot and hit Mongo in the back of the head. Mongo pitched forward onto the table. The tableware scattered. Romero and Bobby Chacon hit the floor behind the table, fumbling for weapons as they went down. By the time they got them out and squirmed into a position to see, Crow was gone.

51.

"Another guy from Miami," Suit said.

He handed Mongo's driver's license to Jesse.

"Carrying a forty-caliber semiautomatic," Suit said. "Full magazine. Got a room key, too. Marshport Lodge."

"Molly," Jesse said. "Get the Marshport cops. Give them the room-key info, see what they can find."

"Armed and dangerous?" Molly said.

"You might mention that," Jesse said.

Molly went to one of the cruisers.

"Witnesses?" Jesse said to Suit.

"Lot of them," Suit said. "Nobody knows

what happened. Three guys came in, sat down, ordered lunch. They're eating lunch, there's a shot. Nobody knows from where. Nobody saw the shooter. The other two guys hit the floor, they have guns. After a minute they get up and run from the restaurant."

"Car?" Jesse said.

"Nobody dared look," Suit said.

Jesse stood looking down at Mongo's body sprawled across the table.

"Shot had to come from the wharf," Jesse said. "No place else a guy could stand and hit him in the back of the head."

"Unless it was another long rifle shot," Suit said.

"Most people on a long shot don't aim for the head," Jesse said.

"Unless it was a lousy shot that worked out," Suit said.

"ME will tell us what kind of bullet," Jesse said. "Meanwhile, I'm sticking with the wharf."

Suit nodded. Jesse went out the restaurant and across the little gangway to the wharf and walked over so he was standing where he figured the shooter had stood. Suit walked with him.

"You think it was Crow?" Suit said.

"Yes."

"Can we prove it?"

"Not yet," Jesse said.

Suit was silent. They both looked at the corpse on the deck. It was an easy shot.

"You told me Crow could really shoot," Suit said.

"He's as good as I am," Jesse said.

"Wow!" Suit said.

Jesse smiled slightly.

"Right answer," he said.

"So a good shot," Suit said. "Standing here. Probably using a semiautomatic with ten, fifteen rounds in it. Why didn't he kill them all?"

"I don't know," Jesse said.

They stood again in silence, looking at the crime scene. The ME's truck had arrived. Peter Perkins had finished taking his pictures and was packing up his equipment. Arthur Angstrom was keeping the sightseers at bay behind some yellow tape. Molly and Eddie Cox were still talking to a huddle of restaurant workers and patrons and learning nothing.

"It wouldn't be conscience," Suit said.

Jesse smiled.

"No," he said. "It wouldn't be conscience."

52.

Marshport police headquarters was in a nineteenth-century brick and brownstone building with an arched entranceway that looked like it might be a library, or a school. Jesse sat in the basement in a blank interrogation room with yellow walls, with a Marshport detective named Concannon, and an Essex County assistant DA named Tremaine. Concannon was a big, hard-looking man with black curly hair and a handlebar mustache. There was a small white scar across the bridge of his nose. Tremaine had short, thick hair with blond highlights, and big, round tinted glasses. Jesse thought her legs were good.

With them was Bobby Chacon.

"We got him with an unlicensed handgun," Concannon said.

"And we called Florida," Tremaine said, "and, to our amazement, we find that Bobby has two previous convictions."

"So this would make strike three," Jesse said.

"If it were a violent felony," Chacon said.

Nobody said anything.

"It's a simple gun possession," Chacon said. "Throw the book at me, I get maybe a year."

"It could be more serious," Tremaine said.

"Yeah? How?"

"We might find a way to up the stakes a little," Concannon said.

"I heard he actually fired at you when you were attempting to place him under arrest," Jesse said.

Concannon nodded.

"That would crank everything up some," Tremaine said.

"That's a fucking lie," Chacon said. "Excuse my language, ma'am."

"And cursing in front of a ladylike ADA," Tremaine said. "That must be some kind of fucking crime. Right?"

"It don't help none," Concannon said.

"I didn't resist no arrest," Chacon said.

"You know a guy named Larson?" Jesse said.

"Nope."

"He's from Miami, too," Jesse said.

"Big city," Chacon said.

"And he was registered at the same motel you were, next room."

"Don't know him," Chacon said.

"How about Estella?" Concannon said.

"Nope."

"That's odd," Tremaine said. "He was registered to the same room you were."

"Must be a mistake at the front desk," Chacon said.

"Guy named Romero shared the room with Larson," Tremaine said. "Know him?"

Chacon leaned back and tried to look contemplative. Then he shook his head.

"Nope," he said. "Sorry. Don't recognize the name."

Tremaine stood.

"I'm tired of this," she said. "He says something worth hearing, let me know."

She left the room. Chacon watched her go.

"Nice ass," he said.

Concannon slapped him hard across the face.

"Respect," Concannon said.

As soon as the door closed behind Tremaine, it opened again and a tall, fat cop with a shaved head and a roll of fat over the back of his collar came in and stood against the wall behind Chacon.

"I want a lawyer," Chacon said.

"Sure thing," Concannon said. "Your constitutional right. Usually takes a while to arrange, though. Probably won't get here until after you try to make a break for it, and end up falling down a long flight of stairs."

"You don't scare me," Chacon said.

"Not yet," Concannon said.

He took a pair of black leather gloves out of his hip pocket and began to inch one of them onto his left hand.

"You want to go outside, Chief Stone," Concannon said. "Sometimes small-town cops get a little queasy."

Jesse stood up.

"Look, Bobby," he said. "You can help us out here and we can probably look the other way on the gun charge." Jesse looked at Concannon, who shrugged. "Otherwise we'll frame you for something that'll put you away for life."

Chacon stared at Jesse.

"You say it right out?"

"Yes," Jesse said, "that's how it's going to go. I stay here, you tell me what's been going on. Or I leave and you get framed and fall down a long flight of stairs. It's why the ADA went out. She knows how it's going to go. She doesn't mind the frame job, but she don't like the stairs much."

Chacon gave Jesse a dead-eyed stare. Jesse shrugged and started for the door. Concannon was wiggling his right hand into the second glove.

"Okay," Chacon said. "I'll tell you some things."

53.

Suit was outside Jesse's condo in a squad car. Molly was inside, reading *The New York Times.* Amber sat crosslegged on the floor in front of the television, watching an inside Hollywood show on E! Amber was bored. She shifted her position, fiddled with her hair, yawned loudly.

"You married?" she said to Molly.

"Yes."

"What's your old man do?"

"My husband builds boats," Molly said.

"Any money in that?" Amber said.

"Some."

"So how come you work?"

"I like to work," Molly said.

"As a cop?" Amber said.

"I like being a cop," Molly said.

Amber shook her head sadly.

"You got kids?"

"Four," Molly said.

"Any daughters?"

"One," Molly said.

"You ever fool around?"

"You mean like sex?" Molly said.

"Like, duh?" Amber said. "Of course sex."

"Might be none of your business," Molly said.

Amber shrugged.

"So did ya?" she said.

Molly thought for a moment about the way Crow seemed to look through her clothes. She felt her face flush slightly.

"You did, didn't you?" Amber said.

"No," Molly said. "I have never cheated on my husband."

"Why not?" Amber said. "Doesn't it get boring doing it with the same guy every day?"

Molly smiled.

"When you've been married fourteen years, and you both work, and you got four kids, it's not every day," Molly said.

"Man, you're as drab as Jesse," Amber said. "You have any fun before you got married?"

"I got married pretty early," Molly said.

"Jesus," Amber said. "Tell me you weren't a freaking virgin."

"No," Molly said. "I wasn't a virgin."

"Christ, I hope not," Amber said. "You think you might fool around sometime?"

"I have no long-range plan," Molly said. "I'm pretty sure I won't fool around today."

Amber looked at the big picture of Ozzie Smith behind the bar.

"Who's the black guy?" Amber said.

"That's Ozzie Smith," Molly said. "He's in the Baseball Hall of Fame."

"So why's his picture here?"

"I guess Jesse admires him," Molly said.

"How come?"

"Jesse used to be a ballplayer," Molly said. "He was a shortstop, like Ozzie."

"Jesse played baseball?"

"In the minor leagues," Molly said. "He hurt his shoulder and had to stop."

"Bummer," Amber said. "And he ends up a cop."

"I think he likes being a cop," Molly said.

"How come?"

"He's good at it," Molly said.

"That's all?"

"That's enough," Molly said.

"Is that why you like it?"

"Yeah," Molly said. "Yeah, it is."

They were quiet for a time. The gossip program gurgled on.

"Must be why I like screwing," Amber said.

"Because you're good at it?" Molly said.

"The best," Amber said.

"My husband always says the worst sex he ever had was great," Molly said.

"What's that mean?"

"Maybe everybody's good at it," Molly said.

Amber was silent for a time. Then she shrugged.

"What's the difference," she said.

54.

Crow came into Jesse's office and sat down.

"Things happening in town," he said.

"All of them since you arrived," Jesse said.

"Think of me as a catalyst for change," Crow said.

"Or the Grim Reaper," Jesse said.

Crow smiled.

"You're not living in your house," Jesse said.

"Apache warriors can live off the land," Crow said.

"What do you do for food?" Jesse said.

"Room service," Crow said.

"Hardscrabble," Jesse said.

Crow nodded.

"Some people in here from Miami," Crow said.

"Fewer than there were," Jesse said.

"They're from Francisco," Crow said. "They supposed to kill me and take the girl home. But I think they handed me off to the Horn Street Boys, so they can concentrate on the girl."

"That's right," Jesse said.

"You know something," Crow said.

"We arrested Bobby Chacon," Jesse said, "and he talked to us."

"So that leaves Romero," Crow said.

"You know him?"

"Yes," Crow said.

"Think he'll try for the girl himself?" Jesse said.

"He's good enough," Crow said.

"But?"

"But he knows I'm around," Crow said. "And he has to assume once you got Chacon that he'd blab sooner or later."

"So you think he won't," Jesse said.

"He's got the balls for it," Crow said. "But I think he's a smart guy. Like you and me. He knows what he's doing. And right now, he's trying to do a job, and I think he'll wait until the odds are better."

"We checked the Miami flights," Jesse said. "He was on one two hours after Marshport busted Bobby Chacon."

Crow nodded.

"You think he'll be back?" Jesse said.

Crow nodded.

"And I think Louis Francisco will come back with him and I think he'll bring a lot of troops," Crow said.

"Francisco gets what he wants," Jesse said.

"He does," Crow said. "And right now he wants his daughter."

"How about you?"

"After the daughter."

"We'll keep an eye on the inbound flights from Miami," Jesse said.

"He won't come commercial. He's got his own plane."

"What kind?"

"Big one," Crow said.

"Like a commercial jet?"

"Yeah."

"We'll check where he might land," Jesse said.

"Francisco has a lot of resources," Crow

said. "He's the real deal. If you had a team of bad guys, Francisco would hit fourth."

Jesse nodded.

"He's got all the money he needs. He's got no fear, and no feelings," Crow said. "I think the daughter thing is mostly about ego."

"You don't think he loves her?" Jesse said.

"I don't think he can," Crow said.

"Well," Jesse said after a moment of silence, "you're right about the Horn Street Boys. Chacon says they picked up your contract."

Crow grinned.

"How much?" he said.

"Chacon says ten grand."

"Ten?" Crow said.

Jesse nodded.

"That what they got for bagging the kid's mother?" Crow said.

"I believe so."

"Lot of money to those kids," Crow said.

"And they're mad at you for shooting Puerco," Jesse said.

"It was nothing personal," Crow said.

Jesse nodded slowly.

"It never is," he said. "Is it?"

Crow shrugged.

"Just thought I'd give you a heads-up," he said.

"Public-spirited citizens," Jesse said, "are our best defense against crime."

"Exactly right," Crow said.

55.

It was 6:30 in the evening when Jesse got home. Suit saw him start up the stairs to the condo. He waved, Jesse waved back, Suit pulled the cruiser out of the parking slot and drove away.

Fast shift change, Jesse thought. *Probably headed for a tryst with Miriam Fiedler.* When he went into his apartment, Amber was lying on her stomach watching some kind of reality show where husbands and wives fought with each other. When she heard the door open, Molly appeared at the kitchen door. She had a dish towel tucked into her belt.

"Nice look," Jesse said. "Is that like an apron?"

"You and Jenn don't cook," Molly said. "And I got bored. So I made you a casserole."

"Is it any good?" Jesse said.

"I'm of Irish Catholic heritage," Molly said.

"Oh, well," Jesse said.

Without taking her eyes from the television battle, Amber said, "What kind of casserole?"

"American chop suey," Molly said.

"Ick," Amber said. "What's that made of."

"Macaroni and stuff," Jesse said. "If you don't like it we'll make you a sandwich."

"I want peanut butter," Amber said. "And a Coke."

"Sure," Jesse said.

When Jenn arrived, Molly left. Jesse and Jenn took their drinks out onto the balcony and sat together. Amber hung around sometimes with them, sometimes in the living room with the door open. Partly with them, partly not. Jesse thought they could probably chart Amber's feelings about them by her proximity to the balcony.

"I've found out some things," Jenn said.

Jesse nodded. It had become domestic,

coming home from work, having a drink before dinner with Jenn. Kid lingering near them.
Sleeping on the couch, on the other hand,
was not so domestic.

"The title to the Crowne estate is a little
complicated," Jenn said.

"Uh-huh."

"The estate was originally built by a man
named Herschel Crowne," Jenn said. "When
he died it was left to his son, Archibald
Crowne. At his death, Archibald left it in trust
for the benefit of some disadvantaged children from Marshport."

Jenn paused.

Always dramatic.

"Being the ones now using the facility,"
Jesse said.

Jenn nodded.

"However, in the event that there was no
use to which it could be put on behalf of
these disadvantaged children, it would pass
on to his only heir, his daughter, Miriam
Crowne...who is married to a man named
Alex Fiedler."

"Aha," Jesse said. "Miriam Fiedler."

"So maybe her motives aren't so pure,"
Jenn said.

"The motives she admitted to aren't so pure," Jesse said. "Know anything about Mr. Fiedler?"

"He apparently travels much of the time," Jenn said.

"Works out good for Suit," Jesse said.

"What works out for Suit," Amber said from the living room. "What are you all talking about out there?"

"The woman who owns the Crowne estate," Jesse said. "She would benefit if the kids from Marshport didn't go there."

"What about Suit?"

"Private joke," Jesse said.

"How come you won't tell me?" Amber said. "I know Suit. He's one of the cops sits outside when you're not here."

"I don't want to tell you," Jesse said.

"Then don't," Amber said. "I don't care."

"You know how much the Crowne estate is worth?" Jesse said to Jenn.

"A real-estate appraiser says eight to ten million."

"How about the Fiedlers?" Jesse said. "You know how much they're worth?"

"No, you think it matters?"

"Might. If they're worth a hundred million,

the estate would be a drop in the bucket. If they're worth a hundred and fifty thousand, it would be something else."

"I just assumed they were rich," Jenn said.

"They seem rich," Jesse said. "Why does Mr. Fiedler travel?"

In the living room, Amber focused deeply on the television set.

"Haven't found out yet," Jenn said.

"Maybe Suit can find out," Jesse said.

"The undercover man," Jenn said, and smiled.

In the living room sprawled on the floor in front of the television Amber was silent, showing in every way she could how little she cared about the conversation.

56.

Molly lived close enough that she could walk to her home from Jesse's condo. It was raining gently and darker than usual for the time of day in late summer. She had put a kerchief over her hair and wore a light yellow raincoat over her uniform. As she turned onto Munroe Street, Crow fell in beside her.

"Evening," he said.

"Hello."

"Who's minding the kids?" Crow said.

"My mother," Molly said. "My husband is in Newport."

Why did I say that?

"Why?" Crow said.

"A boat he built got damaged in a storm," Molly said. "The owner won't let anyone else work on it."

"Good at his work," Crow said.

"Yes."

Crow nodded. They passed the head of the wharf.

"Got time for a drink?" Crow said.

Molly paused. She felt it in her stomach and along her spine. She looked at her watch.

"Sure," she said, and they turned onto the wharf and walked down to the Gray Gull.

"Bar or table?" Crow said.

"Damn," Molly said. "I'm in uniform."

"Leave the raincoat on," Crow said. "Who will know."

Molly nodded.

"Table," she said.

Crow nodded and pointed at a table, and the young woman doing hostess duty led them to it. Molly ordered a vodka gimlet; Crow had Maker's Mark on the rocks.

"How many kids have you?" Crow said.

"Four."

"They okay?"

"Sometimes I think no kids are okay, but they're as okay as anyone else's kids."

"Husband?"

"It's a good marriage," Molly said.

So what am I doing here?

"How's the Francisco kid?"

"A mess," Molly said. "If she were mine, I wouldn't know where to start."

"If she were yours," Crow said, "she'd be different."

Molly nodded.

"Probably," Molly said. "You married?"

"I'm not here to talk about me," Crow said.

"Even if I want to?"

"I don't talk about me," Crow said.

"So..." Molly paused.

Do I want to go this way?

"So," Molly started again. "What are we here to talk about?"

Crow smiled.

"Sex," he said.

She felt herself clench for a moment and release.

This is crazy. The man is a stone killer.

"What aspect of sex did you have in mind?" Molly said.

"You and me, once, no strings," Crow said.

Molly met his gaze. They were silent for a moment.

Then Molly said, "Why?"

"We both want to," Crow said.

"You're so sure of me?" Molly said.

"Yes."

"How can you know?"

Crow grinned at her.

"It's an Apache thing," he said.

"And my husband?"

"You'll continue to love him, and the kids," Crow said.

Molly sipped her gimlet.

My God!

"You ever sleep with an Indian?" Crow said.

"No."

Crow grinned again.

"And I never slept with a cop," he said.

"And would we do this where?" Molly said. "Behind the lobster pots? In the car?"

"Sea Spray Inn," Crow said. "I have a suite."

Molly nodded.

"Would you like to have dinner and think about it?" Crow said.

Molly shook her head slowly. She was aware of her breathing. Aware of her pulse. Looking straight at Crow, she took a long, slow breath. She let it out slowly. Then she smiled.

"I prefer to eat afterwards," she said.

Crow nodded. He took a hundred-dollar bill from his pocket and put it on the table. Then they stood up and left.

57.

Jesse was drinking coffee at his desk at 7:30 in the morning when Healy came in.

"I thought when you made captain you didn't have to get up so early," Jesse said.

"By the time you make captain," Healy said, "you been getting up early for so long, you can't change the habit."

He poured himself some coffee and sat down across the desk from Jesse.

"Solve any homicides recently?" Healy said.

"No," Jesse said.

"Me either," Healy said. "I had one of our

accounting guys look into the Fiedlers' financial situation for you."

"And?"

"They have a net worth of two hundred eighty-eight thousand dollars," Healy said.

"Including their house?" Jesse said. "Their house must be worth three million."

"Almost none of it equity," Healy said. "There's two mortgages on it."

"They are supposed to be one of the wealthiest families in town," Jesse said.

"I remembered you telling me that," Healy said. "So I told the accountant to poke around a little. According to what he got from the IRS and God knows where else, the accountant says that ten years ago they had a net worth in the area of fifty million."

"What happened to it?"

"Don't know," Healy said. "Don't know if they hid it, or spent it, or lost it. What I know is what the accountant told me. They got a net worth lower than mine."

"Low," Jesse said.

Healy nodded.

"How you doing with your crime wave," Healy said.

"Badly."

"Any other help you want from the Massachusetts State Police?"

"I'm doing so badly," Jesse said, "I don't even know what help to ask for."

"Your man Crow involved in any of this?" Healy said.

"When did he become my man?" Jesse said.

"He's not mine," Healy said.

"Lucky you," Jesse said. "Sure he's involved. But I can't prove it...yet."

"Where do the Fiedlers come in?" Healy said.

"I don't know," Jesse said.

"But you wanted to know their finances," Healy said.

"Mrs. Fiedler seems so committed to stalling that school project," Jesse said. "I kind of wondered why."

"And her finances tell you?"

"Her maiden name was Crowne," Jesse said. "The property belonged to her father. He left it to charity, but if the charity doesn't use it, it goes to her."

"And it's worth a lot of money," Healy said.

"Ten million," Jesse said.

Healy nodded.

"If you got fifty million, another ten is nice

but not crucial," Healy said. "However, if you're down to your last three hundred thousand..."

"And you have two mortgages on your house," Jesse said, "ten million could save your ass."

"Nice to know it's not simple bigotry," Healy said.

58.

The man was wearing very good clothes when he walked into Jesse's office. White suit, black-and-white striped shirt, white tie. Everything fit him exactly. His black shoes gleamed with polish. He had a neat goatee and, disconcertingly amid all the grooming, a lot of long, black hair.

"My name is Louis Francisco," he said.

"Jesse Stone."

"I'm looking for my daughter."

Jesse nodded.

"Do you know where she is?" Francisco said.

"I do."

"Where?" Francisco said.

"I won't say."

"With you?" Francisco said.

"No."

"She is a fourteen-year-old girl," Francisco said.

Jesse could hear no accent of any kind in Francisco's speech, neither ethnic nor regional. It was as if he'd been taught to speak by a radio announcer.

"She is safe," Jesse said. "There's a female police officer with her."

"You've been kind to take her in," Francisco said. "But I am her father."

Jesse didn't say anything.

"I've come to take her home," Francisco said.

"She doesn't want to go with you," Jesse said.

"Many children defy their parents. It doesn't mean they should be allowed to run wild."

"You can't have her," Jesse said.

"You do not, I believe, have any legal authority to prevent me," Francisco said.

Jesse nodded.

"Bring suit," Jesse said. "We'll run it through the courts."

Francisco smiled pleasantly.

"Perhaps I will," he said. "Do you happen to know a man named Wilson Cromartie?"

"I do," Jesse said.

"Do you happen to know his whereabouts?"

"I don't," Jesse said.

"Or a young man named Esteban Carty?" Francisco said.

"We've never met," Jesse said.

"Too bad," Francisco said. "I can't say you've been terribly helpful."

"Gee," Jesse said.

"Still, I believe we can manage without your help."

"Is that the royal we?" Jesse said.

"I have a number of employees with me," Francisco said.

"If you attempt to retrieve your daughter, I will arrest you," Jesse said.

"My employees may protest," Francisco said.

"If necessary," Jesse said, "I'll arrest them."

"There are many ways to skin a cat," Francisco said.

He stood up and stared at Jesse. Something changed in his eyes. It was like gazing suddenly into the soul of a snake.

"And," Francisco said, "to skin you, moth-erfucker."

His voice rasped when he said it. They looked at each other for a still moment.

Then Jesse said, "Ah, there you are."

59.

As soon as Francisco left the office, Jesse called Molly.

"Kid's father just left here," he said. "Suit out front?"

"Yes."

"I'll call him," Jesse said.

"Does the father know she's here?"

"Not yet."

"But you think he'll find out."

"Sooner or later," Jesse said.

"Is he alone?"

"I doubt if he's ever alone," Jesse said.

"Should we move her?"

"Where will she be safer?" Jesse said.

"I don't know."

"Okay, so stay with her," Jesse said. "Keep Suit awake. Call me if anything looks funny."

"Yes, sir."

"You wouldn't know where Crow is," Jesse said.

"Why are you asking me?" Molly said.

"Because you're the one I'm talking to on the phone," Jesse said.

"Why do you want to know?" Molly said.

"Because I'm trying to keep track of as many loose cannons as I can. Any idea where he is?"

"No," Molly said. "Of course not."

"Okay," Jesse said. "Where's the kid?"

"She doesn't get up until afternoon," Molly said.

"Jenn left for work yet?"

"She's in the shower," Molly said.

"Stay close," Jesse said.

When Jesse hung up, Molly looked at the phone.

Well, wasn't I jumpy! Maybe I'm not cut out for adultery.

Jenn came from the bedroom wearing a white terry-cloth robe. Her hair was still wet, and she wore no makeup.

God, she looks like a schoolgirl.

"Your hair's wet," Molly said.

"I just took a shower," Jenn said.

"Naturally curly hair?" Molly said.

"Yes. God was kind."

"If mine gets wet it goes floop," Molly said.

"God was kind to you in other ways," Jenn said. "Is that coffee?"

"It is."

Jenn poured some coffee into a thick white mug, put in a sugar substitute, and sat at the kitchen table opposite Molly.

"Amber's father has arrived," Molly said. "Jesse won't give her up."

"Does the father know she's here?" Jenn said.

"Not so far," Molly said.

"You think Jesse has a legal leg to stand on, keeping the girl from her father?" Jenn said.

"I don't think Jesse expects it to go through the legal system," Molly said.

"Because the father is a gangster?"

"Yes."

"That's kind of scary," Jenn said.

"Yes, it is," Molly said.

"Does it scare you?"

"I have a lot of training, and some experience, and I have great respect for Jesse Stone."

Jenn nodded.

"But does it scare you?'

"Some," Molly said.

"Me, too," Jenn said.

"But you'll stick?"

"I am not going to get to the big leagues," Jenn said, "if I run away from a developing story because I'm scared."

"Any other reason?" Molly said.

Jenn smiled. It wasn't exactly a happy smile, Molly thought.

"I, too, have great respect for Jesse Stone," Jenn said.

"And he thinks he's such a mess," Molly said.

"He is," Jenn said. "In many ways. And I have helped him to be a mess. But he's a good cop. And he won't quit on us. And at the very center of himself, he's a very decent man."

"Why can't you be together?" Molly said.

Jenn shook her head.

"I don't know, really," she said. "We work on it all the time."

"When you were married did you ever cheat on him?" Molly said.

"Yes."

"Why?"

"To get ahead. I thought I was an actress."

"And you slept with a producer?" Molly said.

"Yes."

"How'd you feel about it?"

"Lousy," Jenn said.

"Because you'd cheated?"

Jenn sipped her coffee, holding the mug in both hands, her elbows resting on the table, the light reflecting off the harbor brightening the room.

"Not exactly," Jenn said. "I guess I felt lousy because the sex was a means to an end."

"The end being your career?"

"I guess."

"The career was important, though," Molly said.

"I know," Jenn said. "Jesse seemed so complete, except for drinking too much."

"Even then?"

"Yes. And I felt so incomplete...." She shrugged and made a small half-laugh. "Still do."

"And guilty?"

Jenn nodded.

"That, too," she said.

Molly poured them both more coffee. Jenn added the sugar substitute and stirred slowly.

"How come you're so interested?" Jenn said.

Molly colored a bit. Jenn squinted at her as if the room had suddenly become too bright.

"Molly?" Jenn said.

Molly was looking at the dark surface of the coffee in her cup. Jenn waited.

"I don't feel guilty," Molly said.

"You had an affair," Jenn said.

Molly half-shrugged.

"Last night my husband was out of town. My mother had the kids, and I had sex with a man."

Jenn smiled.

"Anyone I know," she said.

"Crow."

"Jesus Christ," Jenn said.

"Have you ever met Crow?" Molly said.

"No, but I've heard."

"And I don't feel guilty," Molly said.

"Except that you feel guilty," Jenn said, "about not feeling guilty."

Molly nodded slowly.

"I guess so," she said.

"So why'd you sleep with him?" Jenn said.

"I wanted to."

"Any trouble at home?"

"No," Molly said. "I am happy with my husband. I love him. I love my kids. I love being married. . . . Hell, I love being a cop."

"Lot of protect and serve there," Jenn said.

"Maybe. But mostly it feels like I just wanted to. He is a very, very exciting man. He seems completely contained. There was no crap about love or anything. Just he wanted to have sex with me, I was a little flattered I suppose, and I wanted to have sex with him."

"How was it?" Jenn said.

"It was fine. He's adroit. I'm okay. And, if you'll pardon the pun, it was a one-shot deal."

"No commitments," Jenn said. "No promises."

Molly nodded.

"No when can I see you again," Molly said. "There was something sort of honest about it."

"One time only?" Jenn said.

"Yes," Molly said. "He wanted to. I wanted to. We did."

Jenn drank some coffee. Usually she was trying to figure out her own situation. This was kind of fun.

"Well," Jenn said. "Here's what I think. I think you did something for yourself, because it felt good. You don't feel guilty about it, so you won't confess to your husband—thank God. You are right where you were before Crow. And nobody has gotten hurt."

"So how come I felt the need to confess to you?" Molly said.

"I think you were bragging," Jenn said.

Molly reddened slightly. She laughed.

"Maybe," she said.

"And maybe looking for a little advice from an experienced adulteress," Jenn said.

"Maybe," Molly said. "What's puzzling me is, I'm an Irish Catholic mother of four and I'm not sure I can find any sense of sin in here."

"Don't let it make you unhappy," Jenn said. "That would be the sin."

Molly smiled.

"I like your theology, Jenn. I've committed adultery, but if I'm happy about it, I can still avoid sin."

"Ruining a happy marriage is the sin," Jenn said.

Molly nodded.

"And I haven't done that yet," Molly said.
"Not yet."

60.

Miriam Fiedler lived on Sea Street a mile and a tenth past the Crowne Estate School in a shingle-style house with a large veranda. Jesse sat with her on the veranda and told her what he knew of her and the Crowne estate.

She looked at him as if he were speaking another language as he talked. When he was through she said nothing.

"What I want to know is where the money went," Jesse said. "You used to be rich."

She still looked blankly at him. And then, almost as if she were merely the conveyance for someone else's voice, she began to speak.

"That was before I married Alex," she said.

There was no affect in her voice. It sounded like a recording.

"I was forty-one," she said. "My first marriage..."

They were each sitting in a wicker rocking chair. Neither of them was rocking. Jesse waited. Miriam didn't say anything. It was as if she had forgotten what she was saying.

"And Alex?" Jesse said.

"He was a year younger," Miriam said, "forty. He, too, had never married. I soon realized why."

Again silence. Again Jesse prompted her.

"Why?" Jesse said.

"Alex is homosexual," she said.

"But he married you."

"For my money," Miriam said.

"Which he spent?" Jesse said.

"Generally on his boyfriends," Miriam said.

They sat quietly in their rocking chairs. Motionless. Looking at the slow unspooling of her story.

"He travels," Jesse said after a time.

"Yes."

"But he doesn't work," Jesse said.

"No."

"And you pay."

"He tries not to embarrass me," she said. "That's worth something."

"Why not divorce him?" Jesse said.

"Then he would embarrass me."

Jesse frowned.

"Embarrass?" he said.

"I cannot stand to be thought a dupe," Miriam said. "I cannot stand having it revealed that I have been married all these years to a man who would only have sex with young men."

"And spent all your money in the process," Jesse said.

"Yes," Miriam said.

It was the first word with a hint of feeling in it.

"If I will give him one million dollars," Miriam said, "he will go away and get a quiet divorce—Nevada, perhaps—and I will be free of him."

"If you had one million dollars," Jesse said.

"Yes."

Jesse nodded and was quiet. The win the ocean brought with it the smell and distance and infinite possibilit

"There is a developer," Miri tin assures me, who will p

the Crowne estate, in order to build a re-
sort. Austin says the town will not prevent
him."

"Austin Blake," Jesse said.

"Yes."

"The zoning board might have a problem,"
Jesse said.

"Austin assures me there will be no problem."

"He's your attorney?" Jesse said.

"Yes. Do I need him here now?"

"I have no plans to arrest you," Jesse said.

"Will you keep my secret?" she said.

"If I can," Jesse said. "You'll need to lay off
the kids at the estate, though."

"I know," she said.

"I'll use whatever undue influence I have
to keep Channel Three from using it."

She nodded. Jesse thought it might have
been a grateful nod.

"What am I to do?" she said.

Jesse took it as a rhetorical question. But
she repeated it.

"What am I to do?" she said.

"What if you got the divorce, without selling the Crowne estate?" Jesse said. "And it
was still done quietly?"

"would at least be free to live my life."

"What would that mean?" Jesse said.

"I..." She stopped, struggling to say what she was trying to say. "I have a relationship with Walter Carr."

"Which you would be free to pursue?" Jesse said.

"Overtly," Miriam said.

Jesse dropped his head so she wouldn't see him smile. *This does not bode well for Suit,* he thought.

"Does Walter know all of this?" Jesse said.

"No."

"Any?" Jesse said.

"No."

"Was his opposition to the Crowne estate project at your solicitation?"

"He was not hard to solicit," she said. "No one was. Out here we were uniformly opposed to a bunch of little slum kids coming into the neighborhood."

"Do you know anything about the Francisco woman's body being found on the Crowne estate lawn?" Jesse said.

"No."

Jesse looked at her. She looked back.

"I did not," she said, with a small tremor of feeling in her voice.

Jesse nodded. And then quite suddenly she began to cry. For a moment it seemed to surprise her, and she sat perfectly still with the tears falling. Then she bent forward and put her face in her hands and cried some more. Jesse stood and put a hand gently on her shoulder. She shrank from it, and he took it away. *I know the feeling,* he thought. *Sometimes you don't want to be comforted.*

"Maybe we can work something out," Jesse said.

He turned and walked down the veranda steps and across the driveway to his car.

Like what?

61.

Esteban was on the vinyl-covered chaise, watching *Jerry Springer*, when his cell phone rang. He muted the television and answered. Three of the Horn Street Boys were watching with him, passing a bottle of sweet white wine among them. Smoking grass.

"It's Amber," a voice said.

"Yeah?" Esteban said. "So what?"

"I'm bored."

"Yeah?" Esteban said.

He grinned at his friends and made a pumping movement with his free hand.

A skinny Horn Street Boy with tattoos up and down both arms mouthed the word *Alice?* Esteban nodded and made the pumping gesture again.

"Don't you want to know where I am?" Amber said.

"I got no interest in you," Esteban said.

"I miss you," Amber said.

"Yeah?"

"I could see you if you promise not to send me back."

"Yeah? Where are you?"

She giggled.

"I'm at the police chief's house," she said. "In Paradise."

"No shit," Esteban said.

He was still watching the soundless television as he talked to her. The Horn Street Boys who were watching with him didn't like it when he muted the television. But Esteban was the man, and no one argued with him.

"What are you doing?" she said.

"I'm thinking about how to kill Crow," Esteban said.

"If I help you, can I come back and you won't send me to Florida?"

"You walked out on me, bitch. Nobody walks out on me."

"I got Crow's cell phone number," she said. "I could call him, ask him to meet me, tell him I needed help. He'd come."

"And when he got there..." Esteban said.

"You and the other guys..." Amber said.

"Ka-boom," Esteban said.

"If I do that, can I come back and not go to my father?"

Esteban paused, watching the soundless *Jerry Springer* show.

"It'll go a long way," Esteban said. "A long way."

"I miss you," she said.

"You banging the chief?" Esteban said, and grinned at the other Boys.

"God, no, there's a couple cops here all day, and the chief and his ex-wife are here at night," Amber said. "They don't even let me smoke in the house."

"Must be pretty horny by now," Esteban said.

"I'm dying to see you," Amber said.

"Set that thing up with Crow," Esteban said. "Let me know."

"Where should I meet him?" Amber said. "He knows I'm in Paradise."

"Okay, meet him on that bridge thing, or whatever they call it that leads out to where we dumped your old lady."

"The causeway," Amber said.

"Tell him you'll meet him there," Esteban said. "He's got no cover out there, so we can come at him from the other side, drive by, and waste him without even stopping."

"In the middle?"

"Right in the middle," Esteban said.

"That's what I'll say," Amber said. "I love you."

"Sure, baby, love ya, too," Esteban said. "Call me back."

He broke the connection and sat back on the chaise for a time with the television still muted. The others in the room watched him but didn't speak. Then he picked up his cell phone, punched up a number, pressed send, and waited.

"This is Esteban Carty," he said. "Let me speak to Louis Francisco....He knows who I am....Tell him he needs to call me....That's right, he needs to....I can maybe give him Crow and his daughter, at ten each....Anytime. The sooner he calls, the sooner he knows the deal."

He shut off the cell phone and looked around the room.

"How does ten thousand each sound?" he said.

62.

Crow strolled into Jesse's office and sat down.

"You know this town better than I do," Crow said. "Is there any place worse to meet someone secretly than the middle of the causeway?"

"The causeway to the Neck?"

"In the middle," Crow said.

"I can't think of any place worse," Jesse said.

Crow nodded thoughtfully. Jesse waited.

"Got a message on my cell," Crow said. "From Amber Francisco. Says she's run off from your place and is in trouble and needs my help."

Jesse nodded.

"Says she wants to meet me in the middle of the causeway as soon as possible," Crow said. "And I should call her back and let her know."

"You didn't talk to her live," Jesse said.

"Not yet," Crow said. "What's it sound like to you?"

"You're being set up," Jesse said.

He picked up the phone and called Molly.

"Where's Amber," he said.

"In the bedroom," Molly said.

"Can you see her?"

"No," Molly said. "The door's closed."

"Go open it," Jesse said.

"Something up?"

"Just go look, Moll."

There was no conversation for a moment, and then Molly came back on the line.

"She's in there," Molly said.

"Okay," Jesse said. "Don't let her out of your sight."

"She's currently bitching about privacy."

"Let her shut the bedroom door," Jesse said. "Have Suit move around so he can watch the windows of the bedroom and the bath. You stay where you can watch the bedroom door. Everywhere else, you keep her in sight."

"What's going on?" Molly said.

"I'm not sure," Jesse said. "Just don't nod off."

He broke the connection and buzzed Arthur at the front desk.

"Who's on patrol?" Jesse said.

"Maguire and Friedman," Arthur said.

"Send them to my condo," Jesse said. "And have them park where they can watch the front door. Molly's inside, Suit's out back. Nobody in. Nobody out."

"Okay, Jesse."

Jesse looked at Crow.

"She called Esteban," Jesse said.

Crow nodded.

"For whatever reason," Jesse said. "You know he's got a contract on you."

"He's an idiot," Crow said.

"To try to kill you for ten grand?"

"Ten grand," Crow said, "is for drunken middle-aged broads."

"We both know," Jesse said, "that anyone can kill anyone. It's a matter of how much they want to and what they're willing to do."

"Got something to do with how good the *anyone* is," Crow said.

"Something," Jesse said.

"I figure she gets me to meet her in the middle of the causeway," Crow said. "Except she doesn't show up, and Esteban and company drive by and shoot me full of holes."

"And they'll come from the Neck," Jesse said. "Toward town, so if we respond quickly we can't seal them in by blocking the causeway."

Crow nodded.

"Her father came to visit me," Jesse said. "He's in town."

"Yep," Jesse said. "Wants his daughter."

"You tell Amber?" Crow said.

"No."

"So we don't know if Esteban knows he's in town or not," Crow said.

"We know that Esteban can get in touch with Francisco," Jesse said.

Crow's eyes brightened and he smiled.

"And if you were Esteban?" Crow said.

"I figure he knows where she is now," Jesse said.

"She would have told him," Crow said.

"And he knows how to get in touch with

her father," Jesse said. "And if I were Esteban, I might call Dad up and say for another ten big ones, I'll deliver Crow and your daughter. One each, dead and alive."

The two men sat quietly for a time in Jesse's office, looking at nothing.

"Why would she call him?" Jesse said.

Crow grinned.

"Love?" he said.

Jesse shook his head. They sat some more.

Then Jesse said, "Are we thinking the same thing?"

Crow shrugged.

"What are you thinking," Crow said.

"That if we manipulate this right, we might roll the whole show up at one time," Jesse said.

"We, White Eyes?" Crow said.

Jesse nodded.

"I don't know much about you, Crow," Jesse said. "And most of what I know, I don't understand. But I know you wouldn't miss this for the world."

Crow smiled.

"Maybe that's all there is to know," he said.

63.

Crow sat on the seawall in the middle of the causeway, talking on his cell phone.

"Can you hang on a couple days?" he said. "I'm in Tucson."

"I'm okay right now," Amber said. "But I have to see you."

"Couple days," Crow said.

It was a bright day. The wind off the water was steady on his back. Across the causeway, the sailboats bobbed at their moorings.

"Can I meet you someplace?" Amber said.

"Sure," Crow said. "As soon as I get back."

"On the causeway?" she said. "Like in my message?"

"Sure. Sounds like a perfect place," Crow said. "Can't miss each other."

"You promise?" Amber said.

"Soon as I get back. I'll call your cell."

"I hope you hurry," Amber said. "You're the only person I can trust."

"Absolutely," Crow said. "Couple days."

"Okay."

Crow closed the cell phone and put it away. He sat and looked around. It was a two-lane road. Traffic was slow. At the mainland end the road curved right, away from the ocean, shortly after it left the causeway, and vanished among the middle-market homes of East Paradise. At the point where the road reached Paradise Neck, at the other end of the causeway, it turned left and disappeared among the trees and shingled estates. Crow looked behind him. The seawall at this point dropped about five feet to a strip of rocky beach, maybe two feet wide, which dwindled from the full-fledged beach on the mainland side to nothing, maybe a hundred feet beyond him toward the Neck. It was high tide. Crow had already checked the tides. Crow stood and walked across the roadway. On this side the water of the harbor lapped against the base of the causeway. He would check it again at low tide. But he was pretty sure that the ocean side was better for his purposes. He went back and sat on the wall again on the ocean side. He looked to his right, toward the Neck.

They'd come from there. This wasn't a smart group of people, but nobody was stupid enough to do a drive-by shooting and keep going into a dead end. So they'd linger up around the bend on Paradise Neck until he appeared and took his place, and then they would drive down along the causeway, presumably at a moderate pace, like everyone else on the causeway, and when they got opposite, someone would open up at him, probably from the back window, probably with at least a semiautomatic weapon. One issue, if there was any traffic, would be for him to distinguish which car was carrying the shooter.

Meanwhile, if they could pull this off, Francisco and friends would be coming from the mainland end. They would have scouted the location, and would know that going toward Paradise Neck was a road to nowhere. But they had no reason to worry about escape.

They would simply drive out on the causeway from the mainland end, planning to pick up the daughter in the middle, and follow the circular road around the Neck and back.

The crucial moment would come when Francisco saw no daughter, and people shooting at Crow. If they could get the timing to come out right, it might work. But it seemed to Crow that it needed tweaking. It would work better if Francisco could see people shooting at his daughter. But that would be tricky. He knew Stone would never let the kid be used as a decoy. And since a lot of this was about protecting the kid, Stone was probably right. But it wasn't all about protecting the kid. For Stone there was a case to close, maybe even some justice thing he cared about. For Crow there was the fun of it. Cops and robbers. Cowboys and Indians. With real guns and real bullets...*Crow's excellent adventure.*

It would go better if there were a decoy. Dressed properly, from a moving car, over a short span, with a kid he hadn't seen in several years, maybe a stand-in would work with Francisco. He looked slowly along the causeway, first toward the mainland, then toward the Neck. It wasn't a long causeway. The reaction time would be pretty brief. This could get him killed. Or not. The uncertainty made the game.

Alone on the seawall, with the wind still steady on his back, Crow smiled happily. Hard to be a warrior if death wasn't one of the options.

64.

In the back of Daisy's Restaurant, there was a bedroom with a single bed, and a bathroom with a shower.

"I lived here when I first opened the restaurant," Daisy said. "I was still single."

"And how is the lovely Mrs. Dyke," Jesse said.

"She's great. And she's starting to sell her paintings."

"Good for her," Jesse said.

"Makes her happy," Daisy said. "Which makes me happy."

"I got a kid," Jesse said. "A runaway, fourteen, I think. Mother's dead. Father's a gangster. She doesn't want to live with him. At the moment we're taking care of her at my place."

"We?"

"Jenn and me."

"Congratulations," Daisy said.

"It's temporary," Jesse said. "Molly can't work twenty-four hours a day, and I can't keep her there myself."

"That would be your style," Daisy said. "Sex with fourteen-year-old girls."

"They're so fun to talk with after," Jesse said. "How about you?"

Daisy grinned. She was a big blonde woman with a round, red face and when she smiled like that it was as if a strong light went on.

"I'm an age-appropriate girl, myself," she said.

"And the wife?" I said.

"Angela likes me," Daisy said.

"Okay," Jesse said. "If I can make it work, I'm going to keep her from her father, and I'm looking for someplace to put her."

"To raise?" Daisy said.

"No, to give her an option."

"And you think Daisy Dyke is going to play Mother Courage?"

"She can work in the restaurant, sleep in the back. I'll be responsible for her. Get her registered for school, take her to the doctor, whatever."

Daisy stared at him.

"She old enough to get a work permit?"

"I think so," Jesse said.

"Is she a pain?" Daisy said.

"You bet," Jesse said.

"Might she run off anyway?"

"Absolutely," Jesse said.

"And you think the town will feel much better about her living with two lesbians than they would about her living with you?"

"I think so," Jesse said. "More important, though, I think it would be better for her."

"Because a fourteen-year-old girl living alone with an unrelated man will tie herself into some kind of Oedipal knot?" Daisy said.

"You're pretty smart for a queer cook," Jesse said.

"I used to see a shrink," Daisy said. "When I was trying to figure out if I should be a lesbian."

"Well, it must have worked," Jesse said.

"I don't seem ambivalent about it," Daisy said, "do I."

"I don't know if this will happen," Jesse

said. "It won't happen until I am sure her father will not present a problem for anybody."

"This is a just-in-case," Daisy said.

Jesse nodded.

"You want to discuss it with Angela?"

"No," Daisy said. "I'll do it."

"Like that?"

"I'm not from here, Jesse, and neither are you," Daisy said. "Neither one of us exactly belongs. And probably neither one of us ever will."

Jesse shrugged.

"And I didn't improve my chance for membership by marrying Angela Carlson," Daisy said. "Of the Paradise Carlsons."

"I think most people don't give much of a damn one way or the other," Jesse said. "Unless they're running for office and their opponent is winning."

Now Daisy shrugged.

"Maybe," she said. "You may recall, I got some nasty feedback when I got married. But you've had problems of your own, and you do a tough job well, and ever since I've known you, you've been a decent and welcoming friend. I love it that you called me a queer cook."

Jesse grinned.

"Can I take that as a yes?" Jesse said.

"You may," Daisy said. "And to prove it I'll give you the secret lesbian sign."

She put her arms around Jesse and kissed him. Jesse hugged her for a moment and stepped back.

"You know," he said, "we heteros have a similar sign."

65.

Crow drove the length of the causeway and clocked the distance, and on the way back stopped to check the water level at low tide. There was a wide strip of sand and rocks on the ocean side, but still no footing on the harbor side. Okay. He'd be leaning on the ocean-side seawall. At the mainland end of the causeway, he pulled into the town parking lot by Paradise Beach and parked and flipped open his cell phone. He punched in a number and waited.

"It's Crow," he said when a voice answered. "Got a message for Francisco."

Crow waited a moment, then spoke again.

"You call him what you want, and I'll call him what I want. Tell him I got his daughter, and I've changed my mind. He can have her if the price is right."

He listened to the phone again as he watched a young woman take her beach robe off near the edge of the water.

"He knows the cell phone number," Crow said. "Tell him to give me a ringy-dingy."

The young woman's bathing suit was white, and barely sufficient to its task, though it contrasted nicely with her tan skin. She looked to be about twenty-five.

"Sure thing," Crow said, and closed the phone.

Crow wasn't choosy about age, though at twenty-five most women didn't seem very interesting. Older women had more to talk about. But younger women usually had firmer thighs.

"It's all good," Crow said aloud.

Most of the people on the beach were women and children. The women generally the mothers of the children, or the nannies. Most of them were a little softer-looking than Crow liked, a little too thick in the thighs, a little too wide in the butt.

Probably not a lot of time to work out when you got kids.

Not that Crow would have turned them away. Crow liked to be with women. And the women didn't need to be perfect. He liked to look at women. He thought about them sexually. Just as he liked to be with them sexually. But he thought about them in many other ways as well. He liked the way they moved, the way they were always aware of their hair. He liked the way they were with the children. He liked the thought they gave to their clothes, even at the beach. He liked how most of them found a way to keep a towel or something around their waists when they were in bathing suits. In health clubs, he noticed they did the same thing in workout tights. It always amused him. They wore revealing clothes for a reason, and covered the clothes with towels for a reason. Crow had never been able to figure out the reasons.

Ambivalence?

He'd asked sometimes but had never gotten an answer that made sense to him. He didn't mind. Part of what he liked in women was the uncertainty that they created. There was always a sense of puzzlement, of tension. Tension was much better than boredom.

Crow's phone rang. He smiled and nodded his head.

"Bingo," he said.

66.

"I need to run this by you," Jesse said.

Dix nodded.

"I'm not sure I'm doing the right thing," Jesse said.

"And you think I'll know?" Dix said.

"I think you'll have an informed opinion," Jesse said. "I will value it."

Dix tilted his head very slightly, as if he was almost acknowledging a compliment.

"I am conspiring with a contract killer, a known felon, named Wilson Cromartie, to keep a fourteen-year-old female runaway from the custody of her father, her mother is dead, and establish a life for her here in Paradise."

"Fourteen," Dix said.

"Yes, and a mess. Her father is a major criminal figure in Florida. I believe he had her mother killed. My guess is that when she lived with him she was molested, though probably not by him."

"Others around him?" Dix said.

"I think so," Jesse said. "I have her a job and a place to stay at Daisy Dyke's restaurant once we have worked something out with the father."

"Can you do that?"

"Not in any conventional sense, but Crow and I have a plan."

"Crow?"

"Wilson Cromartie," Jesse said. "If it works she will be on her own."

"At fourteen," Dix said.

"With Daisy Dyke, and I'll be responsible for her—school, doctor, stuff like that."

"Money?"

"We're working on that," Jesse said.

"You and Crow."

"Yes."

"Have you thought of Youth Services," Dix said. "Other agencies?"

"Yes."

"And?"

"I turn her over to an agency," Jesse said, "and she'll be gone in an hour."

"She might be gone in an hour anyway."

"Be her choice," Jesse said. "I won't have delivered her into the hands of what she would see as the enemy."

Dix nodded.

"Ever have a dog?" Dix said.

"Yes."

"Was it spoiled?" Dix said.

"Yes."

Dix smiled.

"For as tough a cop as you are," he said, "you are a very big old softie."

"That's why I'm talking to you," Jesse said.

"There may be other reasons," Dix said. "But for now, fill me in on this."

"You want details?" Jesse said.

"That's where the devil is," Dix said.

67.

"Francisco will do the wire transfer today," Crow said.

"One million?"

"One million," Crow said. "Wired to your account. When it arrives, I'll call him. He gets his daughter."

The two men stood with their backs to the seawall at midpoint on the causeway.

"That's what you told him," Jesse said.

"That's what I told him."

"You are a lying bastard," Jesse said.

"Doesn't make me a bad person," Crow said.

"Something did," Jesse said. "What I don't

get is, Francisco gives no sign that he loves her, but he's willing to pay a million to get her back."

"*A,*" Crow said, "a million dollars doesn't mean much to him. And *B,* he's Louis Francisco. No one is allowed to tell him no."

"Ego," Jesse said.

"Partly," Crow said.

"And business."

"Yep."

"Power is real," Jesse said. "But it's a lot less real if it's not perceived as power."

Crow nodded. He was looking down the causeway toward the mainland end.

"Something like that," he said. "Timing is going to be pretty much everything here."

"I can help you with the timing," Jesse said.

"I've timed it out half a dozen times," Crow said. "We gotta start Francisco's car about ten seconds after Esteban hits the causeway."

"We'll set up some construction, and have one of my guys directing traffic," Jesse said.

"How you gonna know it's Francisco?" Crow said.

"You told him he had to come himself."

"Yeah. And he will. He won't come alone.

But he's annoyed. He'll want to kill me himself."

"After he gets the girl," Jesse said.

"Yep. He can't let me get away with holding him up like this," Crow said.

"I've seen him," Jesse said. "I'll recognize him."

"Even in the backseat?" Crow said.

Jesse smiled.

"When he came to visit me, I made his car. Lincoln Town Car. A rental. He rented two of them. Got his license plate number while he was driving away. Got the other number from the rental company."

"Wow," Crow said. "What a cop!"

"Ever alert," Jesse said.

"We need somebody at the other end to let us know when Esteban starts," Crow said. "He'll be around the bend."

"If he comes from there," Jesse said.

"He'll come from that end," Crow said.

"And Francisco from the other," Jesse said.

Crow nodded.

"Scorpions in a bottle," he said. "You got enough people to keep them penned on the causeway?"

"I can get some Staties for backup," Jesse said.

"They'll go along with this?" Crow said.

"I may not tell them exactly what's going down," Jesse said.

Crow grinned.

"You lying bastard," he said.

"Doesn't make me a bad person," Jesse said. "When you want to do it?"

"Day after the money shows up in your account," Crow said.

"Time of day?"

"Morning is good, late enough for everybody to get here, early enough for me to have the sun at my back and shining in their eyes."

"Say about ten-thirty?" Jesse said.

"You been doing a few practice runs yourself," Crow said.

"Plan ahead," Jesse said.

They were quiet then, looking at the length of the causeway.

"I need a day to walk my people through it," Jesse said.

"You got tomorrow," Crow said, "even if the money shows up tomorrow."

"Wednesday morning, ten-thirty," Jesse said. "Rain or shine."

"Rain might not be a bad thing," Crow said. "If it blurred things a little."

"Sixty percent chance of rain," Jesse said, "for Wednesday."

"Like they know," Crow said.

"They sound like they know," Jesse said.

Crow snorted.

"Either way," Crow said. "What are the odds of pulling this off?"

"Terrible odds," Jesse said.

Crow grinned.

"Worst case," Crow said, "we got his money, and we're no worse off than we were before."

"Except some people might be dead," Jesse said. "Including you."

"What's the fun in winning," Crow said, "you got no chance to lose?"

68.

The easy late-summer rain had emptied the beach. Jesse sat with Jenn on the bench in the small pavilion watching the raindrops pock the surface of the ocean.

"Can we walk on the beach?" Jenn said.

"Umbrella?" Jesse said.

"No. I'd like to walk in the rain and get wet."

"And your hair?" Jesse said.

"I'll fix it when we get home," Jenn said.

The phrase pinched in Jesse's solar plexus. *Home.*

They stood and began to walk down the empty beach. The rain was steady but not hard. There was no wind.

"So the gang from Marshport," Jenn said. "They think Crow has been set up by Amber and is expecting to meet her on the causeway, where instead they will shoot him dead."

"Correct," Jesse said.

"God, I wish I could use some of this," Jenn said.

"Maybe someday," Jesse said.

"And Amber's father thinks Crow will deliver his daughter to him in the middle of the causeway," Jenn said.

"Correct."

"And you hope to provoke conflict between the two groups and arrest them all."

"Exactly," Jesse said.

"Is any of this plan legal?" Jenn said.

"I may be able to make it look so," Jesse said.

"But you know who most of the villains are already," Jenn said.

"Plus, I know Crow killed a guy in Marshport, and certainly a couple guys here," Jesse said. "Though I can't prove it."

"But you're not trying to catch Crow," Jenn said.

"No."

"Why not?"

"I'm not sure," Jesse said.

"Can you trust Crow in this?"

"Probably not," Jesse said. "And I know that Esteban Carty and the Horn Street gang killed Amber's mother. And I know they have a contract on Crow, but all I have is second-hand information from a known felon, who would probably say anything he thought would serve him."

"What do you suppose Crow is up to in all this?" Jenn said.

"He may be looking out for the girl," Jesse said. "He may have an issue I don't know about that he's resolving with Francisco. But to tell you the truth, I think he's just playing."

"God," Jenn said.

"Crow's unusual," Jesse said.

"And doesn't the father have a legal right to his daughter?" Jenn said.

"Probably," Jesse said. "I got somebody from Rita Fiore's firm working on that."

"And the million dollars Crow has extorted from the father?" Jenn said.

"Rita's people are setting up a trust for Amber," Jesse said. "She stays here and finishes school and gets it at age eighteen. Meanwhile, we support her on the income."

"And if she runs off?"

"I don't know," Jesse said.

"This could blow up in your face," Jenn said.

"I know."

"You could lose your job," Jenn said. "Everything."

"I know."

"For what?" Jenn said.

Jesse shrugged.

"What does Dix say?" Jenn asked.

"He thinks that Amber is probably too damaged to save," Jesse said. "Though, being a shrink, he doesn't exactly say that."

"So you're going to jump off the cliff," Jenn said, "for maybe nothing."

Jesse shrugged again.

"Why?" Jenn said.

"Seems like the right thing to do," Jesse said.

They walked in silence then, except for the murmur of the ocean, and the hushed sound of the rain and the wet crunch their feet made in the sand.

"Be a better chance of all of this working if I could actually put Amber out there with Crow."

"Which you can't."

"No," Jesse said. "Nor Molly dressed up as Amber."

"I could..." Jenn started.

"No," Jesse said.

Jenn smiled faintly.

"Thank God," she said. "I didn't really want to."

"I wouldn't let you," Jesse said. "Even if you did."

"But," Jenn said, "I have a thought."

They stopped and stood in the rain. Their clothes were wet through. Neither of them minded.

"During my breathtaking film career," Jenn said, "I encountered an occasional stunt dummy."

"And went out with him?" Jesse said.

"Not that kind of dummy," Jenn said. "It's a floppy replica, like a rag doll with a realistic look. You know, the guy falls off the building and you see him land on the roof of a car?...What's landing is the stunt dummy."

"Can you get one?"

"Sure, there's a couple theatrical supply houses in town that have them," Jenn said. "We dress it like Amber, put on a black wig with a maroon stripe, maybe, and voilà."

"Better than an inflate-a-mate," Jesse said.

"Most things are," Jenn said. "I'll get it this afternoon and bring it out."

"Thank you," Jesse said.

They walked on. It had gotten darker. The sky was lower. The rain was coming a little harder.

"I don't know," Jenn said. "It may be all wrong, what you're doing."

"I know."

"But it's for all the right motives," Jenn said.

"Story of my life," Jesse said.

Jenn stopped and turned to him and put her arms around him and pressed her face against his chest.

"Jesse," she said. "Jesse, Jesse, Jesse."

He patted her back slowly.

69.

"Suit," Jesse said. "You and Molly bring Amber here tomorrow morning. No later than nine."

"If she objects?" Suit said.

"Bring her," Jesse said. "Handcuff her if you have to. Arthur, you man the desk. If there's an emergency, and I mean a real one, not somebody's cat is missing, you cover it and Suit will take the desk. Otherwise, Suit, you and Molly are in a cell with Amber. Vests and shotguns."

Suit nodded. Jesse looked around the squad room.

"She'll want to know why," Molly said.

"Don't tell her," Jesse said. "Peter, you're on the Neck. Buddy, you're at the construction detour. Murph, you're on the backhoe. Eddie, you're in a car on the Neck with John. Peter will join you when the balloon goes up. Steve and Bobby, you're in a car at the other end. Buddy and Murph will join you. There will be some Staties in unmarked cars in the parking lot at the beach. Commander is a corporal named Jenks. They'll pitch in...at my request...if they're needed."

"And you're in the van," Paul Murphy said.

Jesse nodded.

"At the construction site," he said. "I'll be in radio contact with everybody, including Crow. When it goes down, you wait for me, and when I say so, we come in from both ends and arrest everybody in sight."

"And do what with them?" Peter Perkins said. "We don't have a paddy wagon, and even if we did, we probably don't have enough cell space."

"Healy promised me a State Police wagon, and we can use the Salem City jail."

"Crow?" Suit said.

"Except Crow," Jesse said.

"I still don't get what's in this for Crow," Peter Perkins said.

"Nobody does," Jesse said. "He seems to think it's fun."

"Hell," Peter Perkins said. "I'm not sure what we're getting out of this."

"We might close a couple of cases, and give Amber Francisco a life," Jesse said.

"Sounds like protect and serve to me," Suit said.

"Me, too," Jesse said.

"On the other hand," Suit said, "how you gonna explain the million bucks to the IRS?"

"That's why they make accountants, Suit," Jesse said.

"Oh," Suit said. "I knew there was a reason."

"Screw the IRS," Steve Friedman said. "How you gonna explain it to Healy?"

"First," Jesse said, "let's see if it works."

"You're gonna have to explain this to a lot of people whether it works or not," Peter Perkins said. "We're all just obeying orders. But you're in charge."

"Glad you noticed," Jesse said.

"Healy ain't gonna like it," Perkins said.

"Maybe I'll get lucky," Jesse said. "Maybe somebody will shoot me."

70.

It was 6:15 in the morning, still raining as it had yesterday. Not a downpour but steady. Drinking coffee, Crow was putting on a Kevlar vest in a van at the construction site at the start of the causeway. Peter Perkins had slipped the radio into his hip pocket and was running the microphone and earpiece wires. When that was done, Crow strapped on two .40-caliber semiautomatic handguns below the vest, and slipped into a hooded sweatshirt. The microphone was clipped inside the neck, and the hood concealed the earphone.

Paul Murphy came into the van wearing

work clothes. He poured some coffee for himself.

"There's a crack in the seawall," he said, "on the ocean side. I put a tenpenny nail in there and hung the dummy on it, just below the top of the wall."

Crow nodded, and drank some coffee.

"The timing is everything here," Jesse said. "You can't have Amber up there with you too soon, or Esteban may not shoot. On the other hand, she's got to be up there in time for the old man to see her getting shot at."

Crow nodded. He was impassive as he always seemed, but Jesse thought there was a ripple of electricity beneath the surface.

"Esteban's got to pass this site to get out on the Neck. When he does we'll know it."

"State cops?" Crow said.

"Sitting tight in the parking lot of the post office," Jesse said. "'Bout four blocks that way."

"People at the other end?"

"Yep."

Crow nodded, flexing his hands a little.

"You nervous?" Jesse said.

Crow shook his head.

"I like to go over it," Crow said. "Like fore-play, you know?"

"I've always thought about foreplay differently," Jesse said.

Crow shrugged.

"Romero will be with Francisco," Crow said. "He's the stud. If somebody needs to get shot down, shoot him first."

"You know him?"

Crow shrugged.

"We move in the same circles," he said. "Rest of them will just be routine gunnies."

The back door of the van was open. Crow looked out at the rain.

"Guess it doesn't make so much difference where the sun's coming from," he said.

"Rain'll take care of that," Jesse said.

Crow nodded. He took a deep breath of the wet, salt-tinged air.

"Rain's good," he said. "Rain, early morning, hot coffee, and a firefight coming."

He grinned and nodded his head.

"Only thing missing is sex," he said.

"We pull this off," Jesse said, "you get to keep the dummy."

71.

At seven minutes past ten a new Nissan Quest picked its way through the narrowed construction lane.

In the van, Crow said, "That's Esteban driving."

"Let the van through," Jesse said on the radio. And Buddy Hall waved it on. It drove on across the causeway and disappeared around the bend.

"Peter," Jesse said into the radio, "a maroon Nissan Quest."

"Got it," Peter Perkins said. "It just U-turned and parked near the causeway."

Into the radio Jesse said, "Corporal Jenks? You standing by?"

"We're here," Jenks said.

At 10:23 Steve Friedman said on the radio, "Two Lincoln Town Cars coming down Beach Street. Right plate numbers."

"Okay," Jesse said. "Buddy, you hold them at the barrier. First in line."

"Roger," Buddy said.

"Murph," Jesse said. "Pull the backhoe in front of the van."

"Okay," Paul Murphy's voice came over the radio.

The backhoe edged in front of the van. Jesse looked at Crow. Crow looked back. Jesse nodded once. Crow nodded back. Then, shielded from the street by the backhoe, Crow stepped out of the van and started out along the causeway with his hood up against the rain. It was 10:26. The first of the two Lincolns pulled to a stop at the barrier just out of sight of the causeway. The passenger-side window went down.

"What's the holdup, Officer?" Francisco said.

"Just a minute, sir," Buddy said. "Gotta clear the other end. You'll be on your way in a jiffy."

At 10:28 Crow was leaning on the seawall at the spot where the Amber dummy had been concealed on the other side. The rain made everything slightly murky.

"Jesse," a voice said on the radio, "Peter Perkins on the Neck. A guy got out of the Quest and walked down to the bend where he could see the causeway. He's coming back now, walking fast. . . . He's getting in the van. They've left the slider open on the driver's-side backseat."

"You hear this, Crow?" Jesse said.

Crow's voice was muffled a little because the mike was inside the sweatshirt.

"Got it," he said.

"Van's under way," Perkins said.

Jesse looked at his watch.

"Get ready, Buddy," he said into the mike. "Seven seconds, six, five, four, three, two, one, send the Lincoln."

Buddy Hall stepped aside and waved the two Lincolns onto the causeway. Jesse jumped from the van and sprinted to his car parked in the beach parking lot right at the causeway. He could make Crow out through the rain, leaning against the seawall. The Quest was almost there. Suddenly Crow rolled up and over the seawall and Jesse heard the boom of a shotgun. *Boom, boom, boom,* in rapid sequence. *Christ,* he thought, *a street sweeper. Boom, boom, boom.* No sign of Crow. Then there was a flash of color at the seawall, and what seemed to be the body of a young woman appeared above the seawall and fell forward onto the causeway. Jesse put the car in gear and headed toward the scene. In front of him the two Lincolns spun sideways in the road and men with guns were out of both cars, shooting. Jesse turned on his lights and siren. Steve and Bobby behind him did the same, and from the Neck end of the causeway came Eddie Cox and John Maguire and Peter Perkins with the lights flashing and the sirens wailing.

In Jesse's earphone Corporal Jenks said, "Jesse, you need us?"

"Block the causeway by the beach," Jesse said. "And hold there. Nobody on or off."

"Roger."

Jesse got to the shoot-out first. The patrol cars from both ends of the causeway arrived right after he did at the shooting scene and swerved sideways to block the causeway. Jesse got out of his car, shielded by the open door. He had a shotgun. Most of the shooting stopped when the police arrived. Except the man with the street sweeper. From the van, the street sweeper kept firing toward the sea-wall. A tall, straight-backed man with salt-and-pepper hair walked from behind the lead Lincoln to the Quest, as if he was taking a walk in the rain. He fired through the open side door of the Quest with a handgun. After a moment a shotgun with a big round drum came rattling out onto the street. Behind it came the shooter, who fell beside the gun onto the street and didn't move. The Para-dise police ranged on both sides of the shoot-out, standing with shotguns, behind the cars. At the mainland end of the causeway, State Police cars blocked the road.

"Police," Jesse said. "Everybody freeze."

The tall, straight man looked at the scene, and without expression dropped his hand-gun. The other men followed his lead. Jesse walked to the tall man.

"You Romero?" Jesse said.

"Yeah."

"I'm Jesse Stone."

"I know who you are," Romero said.

"You know him?" Jesse said, looking down at the dead man in the street.

"Esteban Carty," Romero said to Jesse.

"No loss," Jesse said. "You are all under

arrest. Please place your hands on top of the car nearest you and back away with your legs spread." Jesse smiled slightly. "I bet most of you know how it's done."

Louis Francisco got out of his car and walked unarmed to the motionless Amber dummy in the street. He knelt down in the rain and looked at it and turned it over. He looked at it for a while, then he stood and looked over the seawall, and finally turned and looked at Jesse. His face showed nothing.

"I wish to speak with my attorney," he said without inflection.

Jesse nodded. Everyone was quiet. The only sounds were the movement of the ocean, and the sound of the rain falling, under the low, gray sky.

There is no quiet quite like the one that follows gunfire.

72.

Jesse sat with Healy, late at night, in his office, with a bottle of scotch and some ice.

"Quest was stolen," Jesse said.

"'Course it was," Healy said.

"We don't have much on Francisco," Jesse said. "He didn't even have a gun."

"And he was just innocently riding along when a firefight broke out," Healy said.

"We got the others for carrying unlicensed firearms, and for firing them. The claim is that they fired in self-defense."

"And the Horn Street Boys?"

"They got a twenty-six-year-old public

defender," Jesse said. "They'll be lucky to avoid lethal injection."

"Jenks tells me there was some sort of dummy involved," Healy said.

Jesse shrugged.

"And where is this guy Crow?"

Jesse shrugged again.

"Just curious," Healy said. "But you're right. It's probably better if I don't know too much about what went down over there."

"Probably," Jesse said.

"What about this guy Romero?" Healy said. "The one that shot Carty?"

"We got him on the unlicensed gun thing," Jesse said. "But Francisco's lawyer says he can make a self-defense case on the shooting. And I think he might."

"Anyone you can turn?"

"I don't think so. We got the most leverage with Romero," Jesse said. "But he's a pro. He'll take one for the team if he has to."

Healy nodded.

"Besides," Jesse said. "I kind of like the way he walked in there and took Esteban out. For all Romero seemed to care, the kid could have been throwing snowballs."

Healy leaned forward and put some more

ice in his glass and poured another inch of scotch for himself.

"I'm sure he's swell," Healy said.

Jesse sipped his scotch, and rolled it a little in his mouth before he swallowed.

"He's not swell," Jesse said. "But he's got a lot of guts."

"How about the kid?" Healy said.

"Amber?"

Healy nodded. Jesse drank another swallow of scotch. The room was half-dark. The only light came from the crookneck lamp on Jesse's desk.

"Francisco says he'll leave her be," Jesse said. "We got enough legal pressure on him up here, so he might mean it...at least for now."

"She's moving in with Daisy Dyke?" Healy said.

"Yes. She'll work there. I'll supervise her, get her in school, stuff like that."

"Maybe I'll stop by to watch you at the first parent-teacher meeting," Healy said.

Jesse shook his head.

"You're a cruel man, Healy," he said.

"Who buys her school clothes?" Healy said. "Pays the doctor's bills, stuff like that?"

"We have an, ah, financial arrangement with her father," Jesse said.

"Which is no more kosher than this freaking shoot-out on the causeway," Healy said.

"Probably not," Jesse said.

"So I'm better off not knowing about that, too," Healy said.

"We all are," Jesse said.

"You think the old man will let her be?"

"I don't think he gives a rat's ass about her in any emotional way. I think we got a little legal pressure on him. I think it'll be in his best interest to give all this a good leaving alone, for the time being."

"But?"

"But we'll keep a car around Daisy Dyke's as much as we can," Jesse said. "And I'll take her places she needs to go."

"Think she'll stay?" Healy said.

"I don't know. If she stays, she's got financial security. If she runs away, she doesn't. Her mother's dead. Esteban's dead. So she hasn't got any place to run away to, that I know about."

"Talk to any shrinks about her?" Healy said.

"My own," Jesse said.

"And what does he say?"

"He's not optimistic," Jesse said.

Healy nodded. He drank some scotch and sat back in his chair.

"Gotta try," he said.

73.

It was the first snow of the winter. The snow-fall was deeper inland than it was along the coast, but in Paradise there was enough to make watching it fall worth doing. Jenn stood with Jesse at the French doors. It was late afternoon but not quite yet dark. Over the harbor the snow whirled in the conflicting air currents and disappeared into the asphalt-colored water. Most of the moorings were empty for the winter, but a few fishing boats still stood in the harbor and the snow collected on their decks. The snowfall was thick enough so that Paradise Neck on the other side of the harbor was invisible.

"What's in the bag?" Jesse said.

"A care package from Daisy, for supper," Jenn said. "Amber brought it."

Behind them, disinterested in snowfall on the water, Amber sat sideways in an armchair with her legs dangling over an arm and watched MTV.

"What did you bring?" Jesse said to Amber.

"A bunch of stuff," Amber said. "I don't know."

"Gee," Jesse said. "That sounds delicious."

"Whatever," Amber said.

Jenn went to the bar and made two drinks and brought them back to the window. She handed one to Jesse.

"Oh, God," Amber said. "You two booze bags at it again?"

"We are," Jesse said.

Jenn went and sat on the footstool near Amber's chair.

"How is school, Amber?" Jenn said.

"Sucks," Amber said. "Don't you remember school, for crissake? It sucks."

"Gee," Jenn said. "I loved school."

"Sure," Amber said. "You probably did. You were probably the best-looking girl there, and popular as hell."

Jenn nodded a small nod.

"Well," she said. "There was that."

"You like school, Jesse?" Amber said.

"No," Jesse said. "To tell you the truth, I thought it sucked, too."

"See?" Amber said to Jenn.

Jenn nodded.

"You want a Coke?" she said to Amber.

"Yeah, sure, if I can't have the good stuff," Amber said.

Jenn got up and got Amber a Coke. Jesse continued to look out at the snow. Jenn came back to stand beside him. Amber refocused on MTV.

"So much for motherly small talk with the kid," Jenn said.

"Maybe it's a little soon," Jesse said, "for motherly."

"Too soon for me?" Jenn said. "Or too soon for her?"

"You," Jesse said. "You seem a little... avant-garde...for motherly."

"I don't know if that's a compliment or not," Jenn said.

"It's an observation," Jesse said.

"Wouldn't it be odd," Jenn said, "if we put this together someday, and we had children."

"Yes," Jesse said. "That would be odd."

"But not bad odd," Jenn said.

"No," Jesse said. "Not bad odd."

The early winter night had arrived. The only snow they could see now was that just past the French doors, illuminated by the light from the living room.

"I saw where Miriam Fiedler got divorced," Jenn said.

"Yep."

"I thought that was going to be troublesome."

"Guess it wasn't," Jesse said.

Jenn looked at him for a minute.

"You have something to do with that?" she said.

"I talked with her husband," Jesse said. "He was pleasant enough."

"What did you say?"

"He and his boyfriend are opening a high-end restaurant on the coast of Maine, south of Portland. I suggested negative publicity about him spending all his wife's money on boyfriends and this restaurant would not help business."

"God, Jesse," Jenn said. "Sometimes I wonder which side of the law you're on."

"Me, too," Jesse said.

"But it worked?"

"It worked," Jesse said.

"That the broad the cop, Suitcase, was fucking?" Amber said from the armchair.

"Yes," Jesse said.

"You think he's still fucking her?"

"Probably," Jesse said.

"And you don't care?" Amber said.

"No," Jesse said.

"I think it's disgusting," Amber said.

"What I do care about, though," Jesse said, "is that they are people, and that this matters to them in some way, and they probably shouldn't be talked about like a couple of barnyard animals."

Amber stared at him for a moment, and then shrugged and sank a little lower into the armchair.

"I was just asking," she said.

Jesse went to the bar and made himself another drink. He looked at Jenn. She held up her half-full glass and shook her head. The doorbell rang. It was Molly, in uniform, with a heavy, fur-collared jacket on. She had a folded newspaper in her hand.

"You seen the paper today?" she said when she came in.

"No delivery today," Jesse said. "Snow, I suppose."

Molly handed it to him. She looked at Amber.

"Section two," she said. "Below the fold."

Jesse turned to it.

FLA. CRIME FIGURE KILLED

Louis Francisco, the reputed boss of organized crime in South Florida, was found shot to death today in the parking lot of a Miami restaurant.

Jesse read the story through without comment. A driver and a bodyguard had also been killed. Neither was named Romero. No arrests had been made. So far police had no suspects. Jesse gave the paper to Jenn and looked at Amber. Then he looked at Molly. She shrugged. Jesse nodded. He put his drink on the bar and walked over to Amber and sat on the hassock where Jenn had sat.

"Your father's dead," he said.

She looked away from the television screen and stared for a time at Jesse. Then, finally, she shrugged.

"Sooner or later," she said.

Jesse nodded. MTV cavorted on behind him.

"Who killed him," Amber said.

"You're so sure he was killed," Jesse said.

"Yeah. How else's he gonna go? He ain't much older than you."

Jesse nodded.

"It bother you?" Jesse said.

"That somebody killed him? No. He was a rotten bastard," Amber said. "Both of them were rotten bastards."

"You're not alone," Jenn said. "We will see that you're okay."

Amber was annoyed.

"I know that," she said. "And I got money, too."

"Yes," Jesse said. "You do. And no one's going to come back and bother you now...."

Jesse grinned at her.

"Except maybe me," Jesse said, "if you don't behave."

"I'm not scared of you," Amber said.

"No, why would you be," Jesse said.

"So who shot him, it say?"

"It doesn't say."

Molly looked at Jesse, and then at Amber and then back at Jesse.

"I think we can talk about this in front of Amber," Jesse said. "She's certainly an interested party."

"For crissake," Amber said. "He was my old man, okay?"

Molly nodded.

"You have a thought?" Molly said to Jesse.

"Guy had a beef with Francisco," Jesse said. "Took out two bodyguards and the boss in a public parking lot in the middle of Miami and disappeared. We know anybody like that?"

"Crow?" Molly said.

"A sentimental favorite," Jenn said, and then looked like she shouldn't have said it.

Molly blushed. Jesse saw it. *Molly? And Crow?* He smiled to himself. *It's like being police chief in Peyton Place.*

"I'd guess Crow," Jesse said. "Solved a lot of problems that way. He'd double-crossed Francisco twice. That meant Francisco would try to arrange Crow's death. Also frees up Amber here from fear of custody or kidnapping."

"You think that's why he did it?" Amber said.

Jesse looked thoughtfully at her for a moment.

"Yeah," he said. "I think so."

She smiled for maybe the first time since Jesse had met her.

"Okay," Molly said. "Gotta go home. We're cooking supper in the fireplace. It's a family tradition. Every year, first snowfall, we cook supper in the fireplace."

"Hardy pioneers," Jesse said.

"You bet," Molly said, and turned up her collar and left.

The three of them were quiet. Jesse walked over and put his arm around Jenn.

"Molly and Crow?" he said.

Jenn looked up at him and winked. Jesse nodded. Jenn lifted her face toward him and Jesse kissed her.

"Jesus," Amber said. "Can you wait until I'm out of the room to start necking."

"Guess not," Jesse said. "You want supper?"

"Yeah," she said. "Okay, if you people don't start doing it on the kitchen table."

"Promise," Jenn said.

Jesse picked up his drink and they walked into the kitchen. Amber sat at the table while Jesse and Jenn put out the food that Daisy had packed.

"God," Amber said. "Crow is so cool."